THE
BLUE FILES

E. M. Higgins

ORIGINAL WRITING

© 2012 E. M. HIGGINS

All rights reserved. No part of this publication may be reproduced in any form or by any means—graphic, electronic or mechanical, including photocopying, recording, taping or information storage and retrieval systems—without the prior written permission of the author.

ISBNs
PARENT: 978-1-78237-136-6
EPUB: 978-1-78237-137-3
MOBI: 978-1-78237-138-0
PDF: 978-1-78237-139-7

A CIP catalogue for this book is available from the National Library.

Published by ORIGINAL WRITING LTD., Dublin, 2012.
Printed by CLONDALKIN GROUP, Glasnevin, Dublin 11

*This book is dedicated to my childhood friend
Pauline Whyte
1964-1980
Forever in my heart.*

Part one..

Chapter 1

Elliot stood in the kitchen of his moderate and unassuming home. He had been without his wife and best friend now, for almost two years. The only consolation or source of comfort to him, was knowing he had wasted no time in recognising that she was the one for him. He had been twenty five when they first met. He and Greta had cherished all the time God had seen fit to give them. Together with her sad passing and not having fathered any children, Elliot now felt very alone in the world. His loneliness having increased even more so since discovering the truth behind mankind's continued existence.

Homemade lemonade filled the large jug he held in his hand. Not quite as good as Greta had made it, but close enough he thought. It had been a smouldering hot July day. The air now heavy with dust thrown up from the moisture depleted ground. Elliot's house was situated in a remote area of the desert. It had been close to his place of work, and although he no longer was employed there, he liked the isolation it now provided him.

There had been a drought warning earlier that month as no rains had come for some time. Elliot could no longer recall the last time it had rained. The searing desert sun now, conceded the sky to a dramatic full moon. It hung giant and bright in the night sky. The night brought a welcoming cool breeze, and it teased Elliot's face as it found its way in through the open window above the sink, where he now stood. He poured the lemonade from the jug, into an ice filled, glass beaker. Silence now only broken by the sound of the displaced ice clinking in the glass.

Looking out of the window, Elliot allowed his gaze to fix upon a faint light far in the distance. 'It had all started there,' he thought, the world as he understood it over fifty years earlier, all changed after being posted out here in the desert.

The lemonade spilled over the top of the beaker, taking his attention back, although not his thoughts. Humankind needed to know what was *really* out there! Elliot tipped away the excess lemonade from the glass beaker, returned the jug to the refrigerator and went outside. The porch was where he liked to sit in the evening. The scorching desert sun had, over the years, blistered the wood. It no longer looked as pristine as it once had. Not having given it much attention over the last two years, had not assured its preservation. Elliot had no mind to care for it, now Greta was gone, it was of no matter to him.

Greta's rocking chair, as like the rest of the porch, was in a rotting decline. However, the cushions upon it were like new. The thought of his beloved Greta filled his troubled mind. He smiled to himself, as he recalled vividly Greta sitting opposite him sewing and chatting to him about her day. He had always found it quite therapeutic to watch her sew. Now her chair sat empty. The smile faded from his face. Elliot brushed his hand gently along the cushions, then turned, and sat opposite.

This was his viewing seat to the sky above. The answer mankind had been asking since the born of civilisation; *why are we here?* Elliot knew the answer was there for all to see. However, there were *others* that knew this; *they* were the *elite.* The influential leaders. The powerful, but not the known. The nameless, faceless, superiors, not known by such titles as *president, chief or king,* but the *actual* leaders. Those few above all laws, commands or instruction, and Elliot was well aware that *they* existed beyond the parameters of limitations, constrictions, and constraints.

Sipping the cold refreshing lemonade, Elliot gazed up at the moon. His mind was a mix of thoughts, and his heart a mix of emotion. The heavy burden of truth, and his dearly missed Greta. Two of his senses conflicted his thoughts; his sight and his taste, the moon, the lemonade. *They* would not want the truth to become public knowledge, and Elliot knew this. He had his moment chosen, he would soon enlighten the unsuspecting inhabitants of this world.

The ice clinked against the glass as Elliot's chair rocked gently back and forth. The cool night air blew softly against his face. It bestowed a welcoming respite from the hot day that had just passed.

"Elliot Dayton?"

Startled, Elliot's gentle rocking came to an abrupt stop. The ice clinked loudly before settling quietly at the bottom of the glass.

"Yes?" He rested his gaze upon the tall suited stranger, and watched him ascend the four steps of the porch. Elliot saw the gun, and the sudden realisation that his time had come, struck his mind like a hammer blow. *They* had wasted no time. The *Executioner* had been sent.

The shot rang out across the barren desert, and there was no one to hear it. Elliot's lifeless body fell back into the chair, his dead hand releasing the glass. It did not break when it hit the floor, but instead rolled, releasing the ice and lemonade from inside. The Executioner watched the glass as it tumbled over the edge of the porch and down the steps. He followed its path to its final resting place in the sun parched grass. He looked back at the old man he had been sent to dispatch, before kicking the glass further away into the darkness.

Part 2

The Beginning..

Bram's brand new *Buick Special*, raced along the dusty desert road. Bram was very much enjoying its one hundred and fifty horsepower engine, dynaflow transmission and power steering. *Chubby Checker's* new record *'Pony time'* played loudly on the radio. He had had to leave the main highway almost ten miles back, and was now travelling on not more than a dirt track, with only sufficient width for one vehicle. He hoped he would not encounter another travelling in the opposite direction. Bram was now just going by memory, as the map had only gotten him as far as where he had been instructed to leave the highway. Roughly half a mile back, Bram had spotted a sign that had read, *'Restricted Area Keep Out'* and he figured from that, he must be going in the right direction.

There were many tracks that lead off one another, making it vital he remained focused. It was difficult for the most part to know *which* track to turn onto. The dust clouds thrown up from his tyres as he drove along the desert track at times, completely obscured his view, and twice he went off the track altogether.

After some time, Bram caught sight of a high perimeter fence through the dust cloud in front of him. He headed straight toward it. As he got closer to it, Bram observed the fence to be roughly 12ft in height. It had barbed wire running along the top. He also noted that it was *electrified*. Whatever was going on at the Air base was most probably of national security, Bram thought, judging by its location *and* its fortification.

Bram followed the fence line, as he guessed it would eventually take him to the entrance. It did. The large double gated entrance had two guards posted at it, and of course, they were armed, and both were without expression or personality, as Air Police usually were. Bram knew he would not have gotten as far as the entrance if he had not been expected.

Somewhere back on the desert track, he most probably would have encountered these *same* armed Air Police, advising him that it was in his best interest to return to the highway.

Approaching the gates, Bram took out his ID and gave it to the guard that had came alongside his vehicle. The other stood motionless in front of Bram's car, and watched him it seemed, without as much as taking a breath. His work, Bram surmised, too important to let something like *breathing* hinder his concentration.

"Block C is your quarters. It's clearly marked. There will be someone there to meet you," the guard told him, and returning his ID, he signalled to Bram to drive on. "Thank you." Bram waited for the other guard to move out of the way, but he seemed reluctant to do so. After one more long stare at Bram, he moved aside, and Bram drove on looking back at the two guards through his rear view mirror. The one that had watched Bram, still observed him now, and continued to do so until he had turned a corner and was out of the guard's sight.

Bram followed the road markings. Now inside the gates, he could see the Air base covered quite an expansive area. Continuing to follow the signs, Bram noticed in the distance, and at the base of the reasonably high mountain range that bordered one end of the Air base, was a very large *cave*. It seemed to have been hollowed out artificially. Its form, he surmised, could only have been made by machine and not by natural corrosion. Bram was curious as to *why* the Air force should want to burrow into a mountain!

Block C was to his left as he turned the corner, and there waiting for him was another guard, although this one was unarmed. Bram pulled up in front of the second prefabricated building, noting that there were several others. Each was positioned alongside and opposite each other, uniformed in there arrangement, not unlike the houses in a suburban neighbourhood. They were all detached and had been, Bram guessed, erected to cater for the bases' Air crew and their families. However, there were no signs of this at present. Not a sound could be heard, and no one, but for himself and the guard waiting to greet him, were about.

"Second lieutenant Howard, welcome to Air base Aurora."

"Good morning" This was the first time Bram had heard the name of the Air base. It had not been disclosed to him until now. He was surprised to be given its name before the briefing, and in such a casual way.

"This will be your quarters for as long as you will be here."

"I see, and how many others will be sharing with me?"

"No others. Block C is for your use only." Bram followed him into the building.

The front door led straight into a living room area. It was typically military furnished. It had all the characteristics; sparse, no frills, no added extras to give comfort and rest from a long day. Bram expected no more than this, as his quarters at the cadet academy had been much the same. After all, he was not at home with his mother now.

He was in the Air force!

"I think you will find all you need is here."

Bram looked around his new home, "Yes I'm sure all I expect is present," he asserted.

"You are required to be in the *Briefing Hall*.." the guard checked his wrist watch, "in one hour from now." He handed Bram a map of the Air base and pointed to where it was situated.

"If you have any questions, they will be heard then."

Bram took the map from the guard and watched him leave.

Greetings over with, Bram went to his car. From there he could still make out the large opening in the base of the mountain. 'Very strange' he thought, but was sure all would be revealed to him at the briefing.

Checking the time, Bram guessed he had forty minutes or so, until he would have to leave for the briefing hall. He decided to take a better look round his new home. He took all his belongings out of the car, and piled them on the living room sofa. Bram then set to work putting them away.

Everything he noted, was *green*, although of varying shades. The living room floor was covered with a bottle green linoleum. The curtains another shade; a lime green. The sofa was olive green. A small rectangular coffee table, and a large sideboard along one wall, were all that furnished the living room.

Bram picked up his large duffel bag, and headed to the bedroom he had seen briefly when he arrived. The hallway led off the living room. Bram found all the rooms were to his right. Along the left of the hallway were two large windows, roughly four foot apart. Bram looked out of one, and could only see the side wall of the neighbouring building.

The first room was a single, the next was the bathroom, with both a bath and an electric shower. If Bram remembered correctly, next along, was the double bedroom.

It was, and the bed was unmade. A pile of blankets of the type that assured you did not get *too* attached to your bed, lay folded up and stacked at the foot. Bram had recognised immediately that they were made of the same fibres as the ones in the cadet school. The very kind that made him feel like he might just as well have wrapped himself in the same fibre glass material used to lag water tanks, pipes, and insulate homes.

The room also matched the colour scheme of the living room. He removed his treasured double quilted, feather down duvet with matching pillows, from inside his duffle bag. Not leaving anything to chance, Bram had also brought his own clothes hangers, which he now placed in the single wardrobe by the only window in the room. He paused for a moment, and looked out. Nothing but empty desert between him and the perimeter fence, he could now only just about see in the distance. This was to be his home for the next three years. He hoped his new assignment would be exciting and rewarding, as his new environment was positively dull!

With all his clothes unpacked and his bed made, Bram proceeded along the hallway to the kitchen. He found it to be well equipped and *green*. The same coloured linoleum as the living room, covered the floor. All the cupboard doors and counter tops were bottle green. Bram wondered if the person who had chosen the colour scheme, had been trying to, and perhaps a little too hard, compensate for the lack of greenery outside in the surrounding desert.

Bram didn't suppose he would be preparing many meals in there, as the base had a canteen. He had seen it on the map given to him on his arrival. Returning to the living room to take a better look at the map, Bram checked his wrist watch for the time. He would have to leave soon. He did not want to risk being late on his first day.

Examining the map, Bram noted that by the base entrance, and on either side of the gates, were two buildings, one marked guard room, and the other, the reception building. Close by was the canteen, briefing hall and the Colonel's quarters. Block C was one of six buildings all similar to his, three either side of the street and all detached. There were other buildings dotted about the base, but none were significant or unusual for an Air base, unlike the *hollowed* out mountain. And what's more, Bram noted, it did *not* appear on the map.

Chapter 2

Four other Air men were seated in the hall when Bram arrived. All were about his age, he guessed. He recognized none of them from the Air Force Academy. Perhaps, he surmised, they may have graduated a year or two earlier, but no more than that as he knew the first class to graduate was two years ago, four years after the Academy had first been set up.

None of the Air men spoke. Each sat quietly facing the large chalk board at the far end of the room. The door next to it opened, and the base Commander entered, along with two officers. Bram and the four Airmen stood and saluted him in unison.

"Take your seats gentlemen. I am Colonel John Maxwell, and this is Wing Commander Hubert Klaus, and First Sergeant James Wolff. I will ask each of you to introduce yourselves in brief. Give your name, age, hometown, year graduated from the Academy, and what you studied there." The Colonel signaled to Bram to take the floor first.

"Second Lieutenant Bram Howard. Twenty nine, hometown; Fort Davis West Texas. Class of '60. Aeronautics engineer."

"Thank you Lieutenant," said the Colonel. The Airman next to Bram, took his turn.

"Airman First Class, John Harper. Twenty eight, hometown; Bellville Ohio. Class of '58. Social Sciences and humanities."

"Airman First Class Walter Hawking. Twenty eight. Hometown, Jackson Ohio. Class of '58. Military studies."

"Technical Sergeant Elliot Dayton. Twenty five. Hometown, Cold Springs Nevada. Class of '59. Aeronautics engineer."

"Sergeant Bob Denton. Twenty eight. Hometown, Buffalo Wyoming. Class of '58. Engineer."

The youngest of the Airmen, Bram noted, was Technical Sergeant Dayton.

"Thank you gentlemen," said the Colonel. "This is to be your home for the next three years. You have all been given separate quarters and will each be working on different projects. *Do not discuss its details* or specifics with one another." The Colonel was a man in his late sixties with a receding hair line and an authoritative voice. He reminded Bram of his late father who had also been in the Air Force. He missed him greatly, although he had been dead for thirteen years.

Bram had been out celebrating his sixteenth birthday that evening. He now recalled the expression on his mother's face, when he had returned home that night. Bram's heart sank as he thought about what this assignment meant to his mother. It would be hard on her, as he was all she had left in the world. His relationship with his mother had always been a good one, nevertheless it had become even stronger since his father's sudden passing.

"Each of you, is here to do a particular task. You will not be aware of each others work. However, all of you will be working toward the advancement of one project, and one of great national security." Bram now remembered thinking this when he had first seen the base's location *and* security.

Bram had never been in the desert before that morning, and it had brought to mind the episode *'And the desert shall blossom'* from *Alfred Hitchcock Presents,* set also in the Nevada desert.

The Colonel continued, "It was set up fourteen years ago." Bram quickly worked it out, *1947*, the year prior to his father's death. "The project was named *Mission 5*," the Colonel added.

"Each of you will be taken to your *own* specific task area, and an assistant assigned to you. I will remind each of you again, *do not* discuss your work with one another! A record of your progress will be kept, and I will, from time to time, check that each of you are working to your full capacities."

Bram wondered when the Colonel might mention the hollowed out mountain base *and* its purpose. The Colonel continued, "Due to the ongoing tensions with Russia, it is *imperative* that no matter how strange or peculiar something you see or hear is during the course of your work over the next three years, you do *not* speak about it."

Russia had begun testing some very large bombs, and had just masterminded the building of the Berlin wall. Even some of Bram's friend's parents had built fallout shelters in their own backyards! Paranoia was rife. Bram hoped, like many others, that with a fresh new face in the White House, relations between the two superpowers might improve. Besides, he liked Kennedy, and believed in his policies.

Nevertheless he knew the *Cold War* was not about to go away any time soon. "None of you will be part of the Air Base Wing." Bram figured from that statement the Colonel would be assigning them to either, the Air Force Logistics Command or the Technical Command, and probably out of aerial sight; in that mountain perhaps?

"There is no other more *crucial* ongoing project in the Air Force than *Mission 5*. You will safeguard it's very existence from anyone outside the base. *Mission 5,* beyond the base's boundaries, does not exist!" The Colonel added, "One of your duties will be to escort, supersonically, certain aircraft, and in addition you will be required to manage complex air and cyber systems."

Escort supersonically, certain aircraft? Bram had no idea what the Colonel meant by that. The *F-100D Super Sabre* was the aircraft Bram was trained to fly, and to escort *supersonically* any other aircraft, would assume it was also capable of flying level, *and* at supersonic speed, just like the *Super Sabre*. He knew of no other aircraft that could!

Bram, like the other Airmen, were bemused, and looked at each other in bewilderment. The Colonel ignored their baffled expressions and continued.

"Later you will be taken to your aircraft for a test flight."

Bram loved nothing more than the freedom of the open skies. It had been two weeks since his last flight, and he was eager to get back into the cockpit. Nevertheless, he had enjoyed the fortnights leave, and had even met a girl. Although, they would have to settle for a pen relationship for now, as Bram had no idea when he would be given further leave.

"Second Lieutenant Howard, I knew your father, he was Wing Commander of the 77th Air Base Wing. A good man," the Colonel said to Bram. Bram was surprised that the Colonel had singled him out.

"Thank you Sir," Bram replied.

"Well gentlemen, that will be all for now. I will see you during the course of your time here on the base. I wish you all good luck on your new assignment, and again, welcome to Aurora." The Colonel saluted them.

The Airmen stayed standing to attention until the Colonel was gone.

The two officers remained, and showed the new base recruits to the canteen.

"First Sergeant Wolff Sir." Bram could wait no longer to discover for what reason the cave had been constructed. "What is the purpose of the cave at the mountain base I saw on my arrival?"

Wolff looked at the Wing Commander before answering, "That is the Aeronautical Systems Centre."

"*Mission 5*," said the Wing Commander. "One more thing," he added, "the Air police, they patrol the base on foot and in vehicles, from 23.00 hrs and throughout the night until 06.00hrs. You will be required to remain in your quarters during these hours."

"Second Lieutenant Howard, you are to be first to take a flight test. If you would come with me," said First Sergeant Wolff. Bram went with him.

The asphalt surface runway was roughly 12,000ft in length to Bram's right, and 400ft to his left. More than adequate for the Sabre, and even much wider bodied aircraft. With such clear skies, combined with the remoteness of the Air base, and the lack of other air traffic, Bram had predicted his flight plan would be *VFR* -visual flight rules. He was surprised to be informed by the tower, that he was to fly *IFR*-instrument flight rules. However, he knew the best way to demonstrate competency as a pilot, was to control the aircraft solely by reference to instruments.

Procedures were significantly more complex, and Bram just fancied a more relaxed and enjoyable flight, having much preferred to fly solely by reference to outside visual cues. Once airborne, Bram recognized that the IFR flight plan instruction, may well have been due to obstructions in the vicinity of the Air base; the mountains.

The feeling of euphoria, filled his very being. He soared over the desert terrain, his body pushed into the seat, his arms and head now heavy from the pulling G's. The exhilarating feeling of the combined lateral and vertical G's, overwhelmed him, and Bram treasured every moment of it. The loud bang and plume of smoke from the exhaust, signalled to the ground, burner engagement, and Bram was thrust back into his seat once more. Smooth on the controls, Bram leveled off the Sabre and took a look at the Air base and surrounding desert below. The emphasis, now on enjoying the flight.

Bram thought of his father, and how different they were when it came to flying. Bram loved it, but his father did not, preferring to be assigned to the Air Force Material Command instead. In charge of operating the Airfield; maintaining all infrastructure. It provided the base's security, communications, medical, legal, contracting, finance, transportation, air traffic control, weather forecasting, public affairs, recreation and chaplain services. Quite an extensive list of duties, however, none of them appealed to Bram. He never did learn the full details of his father's death. He had not wanted to. It had been too tender a subject. For him, the mortality of a loved one, had been a painful lesson at the age of just sixteen.

Bram's thoughts were interrupted by something he had just caught sight of below him. He circled the base, wanting to get a closer look at the mountain range. Somehow the mountain, he had been informed housed the Aeronautical systems centre, seemed quite out of place, as it stood out from the other mountains around it. Once again, Bram circled the base, and over the mountain. This time he realised why it had stood out from the rest; it had a marker of some kind on the summit. Taking an even closer look, he concluded it must have been put there, as it was far too geometrical in shape to be natural. A symbol of some kind, Bram thought. For what purpose it had been put there, he could not guess. Deciding it was wise to discontinue circling the base, as anyone watching from the tower would find his actions odd, or even suspicious, Bram took a mental note of the peculiar pattern, increased his altitude and continued his test flight.

Touchdown and Bram could feel the drogue chute deploy, which he followed with some serious wheel breaking. Communication from the tower on his taxi back, was minimal.

"*Clear canopy,*" was the instruction from the tower, when Bram had brought the aircraft to a complete stop. Bram released one side of his oxygen mask, as the clam shell reinforced canopy, slowly opened. Assisting him from the aircraft, was the ground based controller. "Why were you circling the base up there?"

Bram removed his helmet, "Just wanted to get a better feel for the location."

The controller only nodded in response.

Disembarking required assistance. The ground controller only spoke again to inform Bram that he was to take him back to the base canteen.

"Where on the base will I be working?" Bram asked him.

"The Aeronautical Systems Centre."

"Where on the base is that?" Bram pointed to the cave, "In that mountain?"

"Yes, the one you took a particular interest in on your flight."

"Like I said I.."

The controller interrupted with sarcasm in his tone, "I know, you were just getting a feel for the location."

Bram had no come-back, as the controller was right to assume Bram was lying, as he was!

"That there," the controller pointed to a large concrete, and windowless building to Bram's left, "is the base's holding compound. Where we hold prisoners and detainees," he looked at Bram.

Bram knew right away *why* the controller had seen fit to point out *that* particular building to him. "I see. Anyone in there at the moment?"

"No, and we would like to keep it so!"

Bram quickly got the idea. But for himself, and the irritated controller, there was no one else to be seen, and not a sound was to be heard either. It brought to mind to Bram, the 1959 episode of the *Twilight Zone, 'Where is everybody?'* which was also set in the Nevada desert.

"Are there many posted out here?"

"All your questions will be answered in due course."

"On a need to know basis," said Bram mockingly.

"*Look,* you know the drill, you *have* been briefed!"

Bram knew he had already made an enemy of the guy, just as soon as he had tried to make him believe, he had not been interested in getting a closer look at the mountains, during his test flight. Without further conversation, the controller led Bram to a waiting jeep and dropped Bram back to the canteen.

"A jeep will pick you up at 06.00hrs from your quarters," he told Bram before driving away.

Chapter 3

Standing in the wheat field, Margaret gazed at the flattened crop. It had a peculiar pattern, huge and complex, and approximately one hundred and fifty square meters she estimated, with small swirled patches and some standing centers spreading outward from it. The farmer's wife had found the wheat laid flat in patterns only moments after it had appeared.

Margaret compared it to the first crop formation she had been sent to investigate just two days earlier. This one she established, and due to its geometrical calculation and construction, could not have been carried out in a matter of minutes as the witness had claimed.

As like the first formation, Margaret noted that the knuckles of these stems had also been bent at strange angles to effect certain shapes in the lay. This could not have been the work of some mischievous or alcohol fuelled prankster!

The patterns, Margaret remarked, were spectacular, with breathtaking symbols. One arrangement had a procession of perfect equilateral triangles from large to small. In another formation were numerous small circles that made up a staggering six armed design.

After having photographed the first crop formation, Margaret had asked her friend Mark, who had studied physics as well as Astronomy, to take a look at them. His assessment had been astounding. By his calculations, it would seem the patterns depicted several galaxy-shaped glyphs, that exhibited a conjunction of the planets as they would appear in the future! Up to that moment, Margaret had not taken the flattened crop phenomena at all seriously. In truth, she suspected her editor had given her the story to investigate, as none of the *male* journalists wanted it. Being new to the job, *and* the only female journalist, combined to guarantee she got the least interesting stories to work on! Nonetheless, what had started out as uninteresting but strange incidents, were now beginning to create a bit of a stir among the local community. Two dozen eye witness accounts on the first formation alone. Unlike this second pattern, that formation had appeared within the space of forty minutes, however, it had also appeared in daylight!

Four of the eye witnesses, reported an invisible force coming out of nowhere, and during calm weather conditions, spinning the crops down within seconds. But still none of the crop stems had been broken! Some witnesses even reported hearing high pitch whistling sounds, and of seeing light phenomena.

Now just a week into her new job, as junior reporter, Margaret was certainly getting to know the local farming people, having interviewed dozens in the last two days alone. The interviewing techniques and shorthand, she had learned in journalism school back in her hometown of Fresno, was certainly being put to good use. Even so, she would rather be following up stories on local politics, or discovering how the town's people felt about their new President in the White House. Perhaps even finding out what effects the new styles of music were having on the local youth. Along with other current issues, such as the emerging hippie culture, the growing experimentation with psychoactive drugs, freedom of personal expression and the widespread tensions growing over the Vietnam war, now in it's sixth year.

These were the topics Margaret wanted to write about. Instead she was in a wheat field, reporting on strange patterned formations! If it were not for the eye witness accounts, she would not have much to write about, except that the patterns had simply just appeared in a short space of time, and that no one was owning up to their construction.

On the other hand, when she began to look further into the mysterious crop formations, she discovered accounts of the phenomena dating back to, and as early as, the 1600's. The patterns of these formations differed from one crop to the next, however, the eye witness accounts were eerily similar.

'An invisible force' and, *'High pitch whistling sounds'*, all these would suggest a flying machine of some kind; an aircraft. Margaret was unaware of there being an Air base in the area. The farmer, whose field she now stood in, confirmed that. Then again, he had also said that there was an Air field out in the Nevada desert, and had added that they tested aircraft there that could level fly at supersonic speed. Occasionally they would fly over his farm. The sound was unmistakeable and was nothing like what he had heard, just prior to the crop formations appearing.

As his wheat field was only a short distance east of the southern Sierra Nevada mountains, Margaret agreed it was very possible military aircraft flew over his farm. He also said the sound was nothing like that of an aircraft flying *supersonically*. It was certainly all very baffling.

Margaret approached the waiting farmer. "I think I have all I need."

"You need to speak to my wife, she saw something real strange."

"Where is she now?"

He pointed in the direction of the farmhouse, "Up at the house waiting to speak to you."

Margaret caught glimpse of her friend's car in the distance. "Tell your wife I will come talk with her as soon as I'm done here."

The farmer hurried off. She walked to the road side to greet her friend. The very same friend she had asked only a day earlier, to take a look at the photographs of the first crop formation. "Hello Mark. What brings you out here?"

Mark looked back at the farmer, "Who was that?"

"Frank Myers; the farmer that owns this land."

"I hope you don't mind, but I stopped by the newspaper office to talk with you and was told I would find you here."

"Is there something wrong?"

"No, no, nothing like that. I just needed to speak with you about those patterns in the wheat field."

"Well it so happens that is why I'm here!" Margaret pointed to the field behind her, "There's another one, but this one seems even more complex than the first."

"Really? I'd like to take a look at it." Mark pulled up his vehicle alongside the field, and retrieved a sketch pad from the back seat. "When you said more complex, what exactly did you mean?"

"It's bigger, much bigger, for a start, and well I'm no expert, but I get the feeling the pattern is saying something; An intelligent design, is how I would describe it."

Mark nodded, and listened to her with intense interest.

The formation appeared through the clearing. "This seems to be the bottom end of the pattern," Margaret told him.

"Wow, it's huge!" he gasped.

Margaret said, "Yes, roughly one hundred and fifty meters square, at a guess." "Indeed," said Mark. "See here how it swirls outward from the center in a clockwise direction," continued Margaret.

Mark was immediately engrossed, "Although some swirl in an opposite direction to the layer above and below. *Amazing*!"

"Yes and these stalks are interwoven, like braided hair," Margaret pointed out to him.

"It really is quite beautiful," he remarked.

"You said you wanted to talk to me about the first crop formation?"

"Yes, after you showed me the photographs, I was intrigued, so I went to the location to take a closer look for myself. What I found was *truly* astonishing."

"Really?"

"Yes, you see here?" he pointed out to her where the stalks had been bent at the base in a ninety degree angle. "A biological anomaly and irreproducible effect known as *noddle bending*!"

"I noticed that earlier too, where the knuckles on the stems have been bent."

Mark exclaimed, "Exactly!"

"You can see the stems are not broken or damaged in any way."

"So they were bent into place with as little force as possible?"

"No, not at all! Quite the opposite in fact," he told her. "That's why I wanted to talk to you. You see when I went to check out the first pattern, I noticed that the affected area of the crop was still alive." He was visibly excited by the discovery.

"All of the stalks remained living, and in fact, had continued to grow despite the interference. Although they no longer grew upward, they instead grew horizontally!"

"What does all that suggest?"

"Well I took some samples of the wheat back to the laboratory for tests, and what I found was striking. I discovered changes in the molecular structure of the affected plants!"

"What kind of changes?"

"The type of changes that would be consistent with the application of intense heat, but for a short duration." Mark smiled from ear to ear. His wide eyes revealing the great satisfaction he felt about his findings.

"Intense heat?"

"Yes," he replied.

"For a short time?"

"That's correct."

"Like what?"

"I don't know," he shrugged. Not having the answer to the question of what could have caused such intense heat, did nothing to diminish the smile from his face.

Margaret looked around at the strange, while awe inspiring crop design.

"Well? What do you think? Amazing is it not?" asked Mark.

"I guess, but what do I write in my article? That some mysterious, and unknown source of intense heat, came down on the crops, and created these strange designs?"

"I don't know," he shrugged again, still smiling.

"The farmer did tell me his wife saw something. Perhaps she can shed some light on the mystery." Margaret surmised.

Mark replied, "Maybe."

"I'm going to go and see her now. Will you be staying a while longer?"

"Yes, I'll stay a little longer."

"Okay, I will check to see if you are still here, after I have spoken to her."

"Sure," Mark replied, now already busy sketching.

Margaret was quite fond of him. They had grown up in the same town. More than a friend, he was like a brother to her. Her middle class American upbringing had not prepared her for the cultural movement era, she now lived in, however Mark's influence had. His enthusiasm for all things new, was very refreshing, and even infectious. Up until she had met him, her life had been made up of her schooling in the week, and playing piano for her parents and their dinner guests at weekends.

After meeting Mark in a downtown record store in their hometown of Fresno, a town surrounded by barren sand plains located in the wide San Joaquin valley of California, they had remained friends. Each Saturday from then on, Margaret would meet him at the record store whenever she could. In the store's listening booth they sang along to songs like, *Nat king Cole's Unforgettable, Johnny Ray's Cry* and *Mario Lanza's Be My Love*. As she was an only child, Margaret looked forward to their meetings at the downtown store. They were just two teenagers, enjoying their young lives *together*.

Mark had influenced her choice of career as a journalist, albeit, unwittingly. He had opened up her world, giving her a thirst for more. Her present job was her first after graduating from journalism school only two months earlier. She had hoped for better, however, seeing Mark again, and knowing that he was now well, made her happy. She had missed him. The emerging hippie scene, and the freedom of personal expression, impacted greatly on the youth. Mark's experimentation with psychoactive drugs, had almost cost him his life. She hadn't recognised the symptoms of his drug use, as she had been grief stricken after the death of her parents. Margaret felt protective over him, even though he was older than her by two years, it did not matter, for she cared for him like a big sister would, and he was the closest thing to family she had left.

As Margaret ascended the porch steps, the screen door opened. "Are you the newspaper reporter come about those strange patterns in the field?"

"Yes that's right," Margaret put out her hand, and couldn't help but notice how stern the old lady was.

"Well you better come in." The farmer's wife wiped her hands in her apron before shaking hands with her. "This whole business is very strange. Why just this morning, I received a telegram from the government, telling me *not* to speak to any reporters about what I had seen. Well I tell you, who are they to tell me *who* I can talk to *and* about what I've seen in my own field!"

It now became clear to Margaret why the old lady had seemed so stern to her.

"From the government you say?"

"Yes that's right. I thought it might have been a hoax at first, but no, it was not!"

The old lady was quite furious. She showed Margaret into the kitchen.

"Please sit down. I have just made some fresh coffee."

"Thank you."

"You're not from around these parts, are you?"

"No, I'm from Fresno."

"Fresno, eh?"

"Yes. I just started working for the local Herald."

"That's nice," the old lady replied, passing her a mug of the freshly made coffee.

"So what did you see? Your husband said that just before the patterns in the crop appeared, you had seen something. Is that right?"

"Yes that's right, I did. But they have no right telling me what to do! Government indeed!" She seemed more concerned with being told *not* to talk about what she had seen, than she was about saying what it was, she *had* seen.

"Please, can you tell me.."

"Harriett is my name, and yours?" she interrupted.

"Margaret Baker," she replied, now realizing this was one interview she was not going to control.

"Well Margaret from Fresno, I don't quite know what to make of it, really I don't."

Margaret began to think that getting a straight answer from Harriett, was not going to happen any time soon. All the interviewing techniques she had learned in journalism school, were not about to work on Harriett. Margaret sat back in her seat, sipped the coffee, and prepared herself for a long interview. She wondered if Mark would still be in the field by the time she finished up with Harriett. She doubted it.

Chapter 4

Harriet was furious over the telegram, "Those are our fields, and our crops!"

"Indeed, but could you *please* tell me what it was that you saw?" pressed Margaret.

"I had been out all day in the fields and on my return I heard a whistling sound."

"A whistling sound you say?" Margaret recalled being given a similar account after the first formation had appeared.

"Yes, but there's more," Harriett added.

"Go on," urged Margaret.

"It seemed to be coming from over head and when I looked up.."

"Harriett!" her husband interrupted.

"What? What is it?" Harriett asked him and was clearly irritated by his interruption.

"Another one!" he exclaimed and pointed toward the field outside.

"Another what?" Harriett replied, now getting to her feet.

Margaret asked, "Do you mean another crop formation?"

"Yes, yes, another one!" Frank ushered Harriett outside, "Come I'll show you!"

"What on earth is going on here!" exclaimed Harriett, joining him outside.

Margaret followed them out into the field.

"In broad daylight too, *and* I just in the field minutes earlier!" said Frank.

She wondered if she would ever get to finish the interview with Harriett. Again she couldn't help wishing she was some place else reporting on more important issues, like the present cultural movement, sexual mores, and even how music was impacting on the youth. There was a new era of drugs and a new found freedom of personal expression. These, she thought, were the current topics and concerns of society *and* not *crop patterns!*

She felt like it was all passing her by. *'Ask not what your country can do for you, ask what you can do for your country.'* Margaret recalled the new president's inaugural address some six months earlier. She wished to be in the thick of it but instead, found herself in some out-of-the-way *nowhere* reporting on patterns in wheat fields!

Now exasperated, "You were saying?" said Margaret, following close behind.

"When you looked up..?"

"Yes that's right, I saw a tornado. Well not a *tornado* exactly." Harriett was clearly distracted at the sight of the new crop pattern. "It's smaller than the other one," Harriett told her husband. "Much smaller."

"Here's your friend," Frank said to Margaret. Mark was running toward them.

"I heard a loud whooshing sound coming from this vicinity!" He told them.

"Came as quick as I could. Was very loud, like an aircraft. Anyone see anything?" He looked round and saw the newly formed pattern. "Wow, when did that appear?"

Harriett answered, "Just a few minutes ago."

Mark looked round the small group now gathered in the field, "Anybody see what made it?"

"No. Nothing," Frank replied. All the others just shook their heads that they hadn't either.

Mark declared, "This one makes *three* in under a week!"

"What I want to know is *who* is going to do something about it?" stated Harriett.

"What I don't understand, is how this can happen in broad daylight, and no one seen a thing!" said Frank.

"Well they better not think that they can send me another one of their *telegrams*!" Harriett bellowed. "And our son out there in that god unholy place!"

"Where is your son?" Margaret inquired.

"Vietnam," Frank answered.

"Been there close to two years now," said Harriett, now visibly upset.

Margaret quickly realised what the arrival of the telegram must have meant to Harriett. "Would you like to finish our interview tomorrow?"

"Yes, yes, tomorrow would be better," Harriett wiped the tears from her eyes. Frank put his arm around her and lead her in the direction of the farmhouse.

"You okay Mark?" asked Margaret.

"Yes I'm fine," He was now busy sketching the new pattern.

"Got more to tell you."

"Really?"

"Oh yes. That's why I came out here."

"Oh right, you did say earlier. What is it you wanted to tell me?"

"Let me show you instead." Mark turned the pages of the notepad he had been using to sketch in. "Here! This is the one!"

"That's part of the first crop formation if I'm not mistaken."

"Yes that's right," Mark replied.

"What about it?"

"Have you ever seen pictures of those symbols found in the tombs of Egypt?"

"Why, yes I have."

"Well do you see any similarities?" He gave her the sketch pad. "They look alike, don't you think?"

"I guess it does bring to mind Egyptian hieroglyphics," she agreed.

"This cancels out any chance of these patterns being carried out by pranksters!"

Margaret asked, "How can you be sure?"

"*Intelligent* design! Just like you said!" Mark bent down and pulled a wheat stem out of the ground. "That's not the only thing I discovered," Mark continued. "You see the pressure that created these patterns, could only have occurred in a matter of seconds!"

"How do you know this?"

"Because any longer would have resulted in damage to the crop! And there was none!" He showed her the undamaged stem. He was clearly excited.

"Yes, you said the affected crop had continued to grow."

"That's right," he answered.

"That leaves us back to *what* could have created these formations, and *so* instantaneously! So what could have done that?"

"Don't know," shrugged Mark.

Margaret was left with more questions now than ever! She needed some time to think.

"We'll leave it for the today. I'll come back and to speak with Harriett tomorrow morning," she told him.

"I brought my camping equipment with me and will be staying here for the night."

Surprised by this, Margaret asked, "What for?"

"To see if I might catch sight of whatever is responsible for creating these crop formations. I'll set up camp just over there," he showed her.

"Alright, I guess I can't change your mind."

"No. I'll be fine. It's been a long time since I went camping though!"

"I'm sure you know what you're doing," she smiled to him. "I'll check in on you in the morning," she added and left.

That night, and after putting together a rough draft for her article, Margaret had fallen asleep. The noise of the alarm woke her from her dream. For that she was grateful, for it hadn't been a particularly nice dream. Now fully awake, she could not recall what exactly it had been about. She got herself ready and left for the Myers farm, deciding to check in with Mark before speaking to Harriett.

On her way, she passed the field where the first of the peculiar formations had appeared. Since then, the mysterious patterns had become even more of a mystery. She couldn't help but wonder about what Mark had told her. She would include his findings in her article, she determined. Mark's expertise and knowledge helped lend credence to how peculiar the crop patterns were. Although she had no real answers to the question of *what* had made them, however, she was sure of one thing, what Mark had discovered, ruled out any human element. Now the mystery really begins! She told herself.

Mark was not at the campsite. Unable to find him, and figuring he was most likely about somewhere taking samples and sketching, she headed to the Myers farmhouse to speak with Harriett.

A few yards from the farmhouse, Margaret could see Harriett on the porch sweeping. "Morning Harriett."

"Oh, good morning," said Harriett. "Here to finish our interview then?" Harriett put aside the broom, and waited for Margaret to ascend the porch steps.

"Yes. Maybe we'll get it done this time," Margaret smiled.

Smiling back, Harriett answered, "Indeed we just might. Come on in."

Margaret couldn't help but notice, that Harriett was in a much better mood than she had been the day before.

"Frank is down in the fields with your friend."

"Oh right. I stopped by his tent on my way here, but didn't see him. I'll catch him when we're done," she told Harriett.

"Oh no need. He will be here soon, for his breakfast."

"I see." Mark was such as nice guy, and Margaret was not surprised that Harriett should want to mother him. He had that effect on older ladies, especially those who were mothers themselves.

"Yes, can't have a young lad like that missing his breakfast. My son is about his age."

"He's in Vietnam, you said," Margaret recalled how upset Harriett had been the day before.

"Yes, my Tom. He'll have been over there two years next month."

"You must miss him."

"Very much!"

"Have you any other children?" Margaret followed Harriett to the kitchen.

"No, no other children," answered Harriet.

"Would you like to tell me more about what you saw just prior to the patterns appearing?" Margaret quickly asked, wanting to get the interview over with as soon as possible.

"Yes of course. Like I was saying, I heard this loud sort of whistling sound. It seemed to be coming from over head. When I looked up I saw a., well a dark funnel-shaped cloud! Shaped like a tornado."

"Was it a tornado, do you think?"

"No it wasn't, but that's the only way I can describe it really. Except that it was shorter, much shorter than tornado funnels usually are.

"Shorter, you say?" Margaret wrote it all down.

"Yes. It didn't touch the ground, it was high in the sky, and stranger still, it wasn't moving!"

"It didn't move?"

"No! Not at all. It was as if it had been painted into the heavens!" Harriett explained.

"How long was it there for?"

"That's the thing, even though I no longer heard the whistling noise, the dark funnel shape remained in the sky for nearly an hour!"

"When did the pattern in your wheat field appear relevant to you hearing the noise?"

"I was on my way back from the field, after bringing Frank some coffee. He was down there checking on some fencing. When I heard the noise, I went back down to check on Frank, and there they were! The patterns in the wheat!"

"So your husband saw the tornado shape in the sky too?"

"Yes!"

"And it was there for almost an hour?"

"Yes that's right," answered Harriett adding, "What do you make of it?"

"I don't know."

"Neither do I. But I will say this, it is all very odd. Very odd indeed!"

"Yes, it is strange," Margaret agreed.

The back door opened, it was Frank, and Mark was with him. Margaret stopped writing. "Good morning Mark. How was your night? Did you see anything?"

"Morning Margaret. No, saw nothing. Checked the fields at daylight too, but there were no new patterns."

"Well that's good to hear!" declared Harriett. "Come sit down and have some breakfast young man."

"I'm about finished here," said Margaret, pushing her chair from the table.

"You leaving now?" Mark asked her.

Margaret rose from her seat. "Yes, got to go to the office and write up this article for tomorrows paper."

"So it will be in the morning paper? I'll look forward to reading it!" said Mark .

"Well, you be sure to mention in your story, that us farmers won't be told what we can and can't say about what happens on our own land!" Harriett told her.

"Yes of course. What are your plans Mark? Are you heading back to town?"

"No, no I'm going to stay here for one more night."

"Oh right. You really are interested in this."

"Oh yes, very much so."

"Well alright, I'll drop by in the morning and see how your night went."

"Okay that's fine. See you then."

"We'll look after him," Harriett assured her.

Margaret smiled at him, "See you tomorrow morning then."

"Oh Margaret, before you go, do you remember my friend Mel?" Mark asked.

"Yes I do. He doesn't live far from here, if I recall correctly."

"Yes, that's right. I got him to take a look at the sketching I made of those symbols.

You know, the ones I showed you yesterday?"

"The ones that looked like Egyptian hieroglyphics?"

"Yes those. Mel's a cryptologist, and I thought he maybe able to make some sense of them."

"Oh, I see, and could he?" she asked.

"The *conduit* is coming!"

"What?"

"That's what those symbols translated into! And if you look up *conduit* in the dictionary, you will find; conveyor of information: somebody or something that conveys information, *especially* in secret," Mark explained.

"And he's *sure* that is what the symbols mean?"

"Absolutely!"

"Well, there is certainly a lot to put into my article."

"I gave him some more to look at."

"What did he say about *them*?"

"He hasn't had time to look at them yet."

"When he has, let me know."

"Yes I will, and don't forget to mention too, about that first formation, and its galaxy shaped glyphs!" Mark reminded her. "I'll come by your office in the morning," he added, as she left.

Chapter 5

Bram had been ready for quite a while before the jeep arrived to pick him up, not having slept very well that night. He recognised the driver, it was First Sergeant Wolff. "Good morning lieutenant. I trust you had a restful night."

Bram got into the jeep, "Not particularly."

"You'll settle in soon enough." They headed for the cave in the mountain without any further conversation.

Upon entering the excavated limestone mountain, Bram immediately was taken aback by the beehive of activity within there. So many people scurrying about from one corridor to another. Some in Air Force uniform, and others in civilian attire. "So this is where everyone is!" declared Bram.

The wide, and surprisingly bright common area of the cave, was vast. Bram guessed that two heavy bomber B52's, and even with their combined wingspans of 370ft, could easily fit alongside one another in the main opening. Height would be no problem either, as the mountain had been excavated to an approximate height of 100ft. It must have taken some time to hollow out, Bram surmised. He noted the many tunnelled out passageways and corridors that lead off the common area.

Pulling alongside one of them, the Sergeant said, "This is where we part company. The lieutenant there, will take you on from here."

Bram's door opened. "If you'll follow me Sir," the lieutenant instructed Bram.

"Thanks for the ride!" Bram closed the jeep door and joined the lieutenant. "So this is where it's all happening!"

The lieutenant ignored his remark, "Here is your *pass*. Don't lose it! You will be required to show this each time you enter the Mission 5 facility."

"This is Mission 5?"

"Yes it is. However, you only have access to *your* assigned area."

"Which is?"

The lieutenant stopped at the entry to a corridor marked, *Lunar 1*. "Here," he replied. He showed his pass to the guard. "You are reminded not to discuss your assigned task to anyone on or off the base, with the exception of those in command of your duties. The consequence is court marshal and *Leavenworth*! Understood?"

Bram acknowledged that he did. The secrecy surrounding Mission 5 was, by now, quite apparent to him.

"Your pass Sir?" the guard asked Bram.

"Oh, yes," he showed it to the guard and followed the lieutenant into the corridor.

At the end of the white chalky corridor was a security door. The lieutenant keyed in a code and the door unlocked. They entered a small room with another security door leading off it, and on a table were white overalls and surgical masks, like those worn by surgeons in an operating theatre. "Here, put these on," he told Bram, passing him a pair of the white overalls and one of the masks. "Suit up!" he instructed. "No need to put on the mask yet."

Both ready, the lieutenant keyed in the code to the next door and they entered the room beyond.

The room had been darkened. The *being* was barely illuminated by a small lamp close to it. Two men with their masks on, sat at the table either side of the being. And standing in the shadows and barely visible, was Colonel Maxwell.

The lieutenant reminded Bram, "Remember, this is classified from the very top!"

"Yes. Yes, I can see why!"

"This way," he instructed Bram.

Bram asked, "What are my duties?" He stared at the being. He couldn't suppose *what* his assignment might be, now seeing *what* was in the room!

"You will sit in for all the interviews, and take notes on any technical references."

"Technical references?"

The lieutenant replied, "Yes. You will be instructed when to take notes and when not to!"

"Where did it come from?"

"That's not important. All your notes must be given to the room commander before leaving this secure area."

The Colonel stepped out of the shadows and removed his mask, "Lieutenant Howard."

"Colonel Maxwell Sir," Bram saluted him.

"I trust the lieutenant here has briefed you."

"Yes Sir. He has."

"Good. The interview will resume shortly. He's a little distressed at present. The Colonel looked back at the being.

Bram nodded, and looked past the commander's shoulder at the being. His large head lolled forward and to one side. It was obvious to Bram, it was having trouble breathing.

The Colonel turned his attention back to Bram, "A grey. Crossed into our dimension.

They sometimes do. When it happens we take full advantage of it."

"I see," but he didn't see! Bram had no idea what the Colonel was talking about!

"He summoned the medical team. Should be here any minute," said the Colonel.

Bram was surprised by his own lack of words. For years he had prepared himself for an assignment on the desert base, but now he was here, he couldn't bring himself to say very much at all!

"When they're done, we can get on. We haven't much time."

Finally he found his voice again, "Is it dying?"

"Yes. We don't have much time," answered the Colonel.

The medical teamed arrived at it's side.

Bram asked, "What's it dying from?"

The Colonel corrected him, "You can refer to him as *he*."

"Yes Sir. What is *he* dying from?"

"*Terricolous Fungi*."

"What's that?"

"It's a fungus that inhabits desert regions. Our lungs contain macrophages that attack and destroy the spores. Their lungs do not," the Colonel explained.

"And can he be saved?"

"Without a lung transplant, *and* from one of his own kind? No, he can not!"

Bram looked at the medical team attending to the being. Their faces were covered with surgical masks also. It was hard to even determine if they were male or female in the dimly lit room.

The Colonel continued to explain, "Fungal spores exist in all environments, however, more so in humid conditions. They simply survive longer when the spore numbers are low."

The being had recovered slightly, his head no longer slumped on it's chest.

Bram attempted to alleviate his unease, "So *H.G.Wells* was right then!"

"*H.G.Wells?*" asked the lieutenant.

"*War of the Worlds,*" Bram answered.

"Indeed." The Colonel was not amused. "This is a very serious assignment. And is no place for cheap gags!"

"Yes Sir. Sorry Sir."

"We're ready Sir," said one of the men sitting by the being at the table. The medical team left the room.

"Before we begin, I must warn you to clear your mind of everything other than what you are here to do! Is that understood?" the Colonel told Bram.

"Yes Sir," 'That would be easy,' Bram thought. 'Who could possibly think of anything else when face to face with an *alien*!'

The lieutenant gave Bram a file and instructed him to keep all notes in it.

They took their seats around the table and the interview resumed. Bram sat opposite the being. It's wheezing was now clearly audible, and he couldn't help feeling sorry for the wretched creature.

Chapter 6

The day had passed without any word from Mark. He had told her he would drop by her office that morning. She had expected to hear from him, and particularly from the Myers, regarding her report in the morning paper about the bizarre crop patterns. But she had heard nothing from any of them.

After finishing up in the office at 5pm, Margaret headed for the Myer's farm, and to the field where Mark had set up camp. When she arrived, he was nowhere to be seen. Thinking that he was most probably being fussed over by Harriett, Margaret left the deserted campsite and headed for the farmhouse.

On ascending the porch steps, Margaret immediately saw the now partially attached screen door. On closer look it was obvious that it had been forced from its hinges. The front door was open, but it too, just like the screen, was only attached to its frame by one hinge. Margaret called out, "Mark? Harriett? Anyone there?"

There was silence as she approached the open door. Margaret had an uneasy feeling and knew instinctively, that all was not well. "Hello? Harriett?" No answer. She entered the farmhouse. "Mark? Are you there?" Still nothing. She walked along the hallway to the back of the house, "Anyone home?"

With every passing moment, Margaret grew more concerned. She glanced into the living room, but could see at once, no one was in there. Now along the hallway again, she approached the kitchen. "Mark are you in there?" She slowly opened the door, "Mark? Harriett?" Seated at the kitchen table and looking up at the ceiling, was Harriett. Frank sat opposite, and although his back was turned toward her, she recognized it was him. She entered the kitchen and walked toward them. "Hello Harriett, have you seen." Margaret suddenly realized Harriet was dead and a scream escaped her. Now only inches from Harriet, it was obvious that she had been murdered! It had first seemed to her, upon entering the kitchen, that Harriett had been looking up at the ceiling, but now standing next to her, Margaret could see that Harriett's head had been horribly twisted straight up, and to one side. Her neck most probably broken! Her lifeless eyes were wide and open, and her face revealed the horrors she had witnessed prior to her gruesome death.

She turned to look at Frank, "Oh god!" she cried out, as she saw Frank's face. His bottom jaw had been cut right back. His mouth now horridly gapping, and without a tongue! His eyes too were gone, and Margaret's knees buckled under her as the dark empty sockets seemed to look straight through her, even though now devoid of eyes. She grabbed the edge of the table to steady herself. It rocked, and Frank's and Harriett's rigid dead bodies hit the floor.

Hastily, Margaret recoiled in abhorrence, wanting to put as much ground as possible between her and the repulsive scene. With the corpses' now laying on the floor, Margaret flinched as she saw the full horror of their attack. Both had been cut open from the navel down, exposing the *now* empty space where organs *used* to be! Her stomach could no longer hold out, and she began to retch violently.

She ran from the house, through the hallway and out onto the porch, where she collided with a uniformed stranger. "What's your hurry?" When she turned to run from him, he dropped his duffle bag and grabbed hold of her by both shoulders, " I asked you, what's *your* hurry!" Now noticing the damaged doors, "What's going on here?" He squeezed Margaret's shoulders tighter. "Are you *going* to tell me?" He turned to the open door and called into the house, "Mom? Are you okay? It's Tom. I'm home."

"Tom," she noticed the *US Army* tag on the duffle bag by his feet; he had returned from his tour of duty in Vietnam.

"Oh my god.. *You're* Harriett's son.." barely getting the words out. "I'm so sorry.."

"Yes I am. Who are you?" He glanced over at the door again, "And what happened to the door?"

"I. I'm so sorry, I.." she tried desperately to free herself from his grip on her.

"Sorry for *what*? What the *hell* is going on here?" he bellowed.

"They've been murdered.."

"Who? Who's been murdered?"

"Harriett, I mean your parents.."

He threw her aside, "Don't you go *anywhere*!" He pointed at her, "You better still *be here* when I return!" He entered the house.

"No. don't go in there!" He was already inside. Margaret took deep breaths of the cool evening air, hoping to stop the spasms in her stomach. Seconds passed like minutes. There was silence. She looked intently at the door waiting for him to return, but nothing; there was no sign of him. Cautiously she approached the open door, reluctant to go in. "Hello. Are you okay?" Of course she knew he would not be okay after seeing his parents' lifeless bodies, and they having been mutilated in that way!

But she could think of nothing else to say. Not the homecoming he had planned!

Finally he emerged from the house, his facial expression revealing the repulsion at what he had seen. He stumbled, Margaret moved closer to him, catching his arm, "Sit down." She lead him to the porch steps, "Sit here a minute."

"Who has done this?" He was dazed.

"I don't know. I came out to see them and found.."

He tried to get up but stumbled, "Who are you?"

"Please, you've had a terrible shock. Try.."

He interrupted, "Just tell me *who* you are!"

"Margaret Baker is my name. I'm a journalist for the local Herald." Her stomach finally settling down, "Your father called the newspaper office after speaking with the sheriff about some patterns that had appeared in his field.."

"*Patterns?*"

"Yes. I came to do an interview.."

"But what's that got to do with.." he put his hands up to his face, "I mean who would do such a thing?"

"We need to call the sheriff," she told him.

While they waited for the sheriff to arrive, Margaret told him about the patterns in the crops, and about how her friend Mark, who was now missing, had come out to the farm to help discover who or what was responsible for creating them. He listened, but said nothing.

Chapter 7

When Margaret arrived at the sheriff's office the following morning, Tom was already there. She wanted to know what was being done to find her missing friend, and Tom wanted answers to his parent's brutal murders.

The sheriff told Tom, "Devil worshipers!"

"What?" bellowed Tom at the sheriff.

"There's been reports of a cult.."

Tom interrupted him, "What the *hell* has a cult got to do with their murders?"

"That's what I'm trying to explain. You see a little time ago, Dugan's old farm came up for sale, a group of hippies bought it and moved in. I arrested one of their children for stealing from Betty's sweet store. Took him up there to talk with his parents." He shook his head, "Strange I can tell you. All those people up there, and none of them holding down a job." Shaking his head again, "Must be twenty of them up on that farm! I mean what do you think they're all living off? Crime! That's what!"

Tom's patience with the back-water sheriff was running thin, "Look sheriff.."

"I know what you're thinking, but I tell you, those people *are* strange!" the sheriff continued.

"*Strange,* probably, but to kill and to do that to their victims.." Margaret stopped and looked at Tom, realising her insensitivity. "Sorry Tom."

"How do you jump from petty sweet stealing to murder?" bellowed Tom at the sheriff, having not acknowledged Margaret's apology. "Has the coroner's report arrived?"

"Yes, it's on my desk," replied the sheriff as he picked it up.

Tom snatched it from his hands, "Have you read *this* yet?" He opened the file. "What the..," His eyes wide with disbelief.

"These satanic groups are said to remove their victims' sex organs, eyes and tongues, for their rituals." The sheriff looked at Margaret, "Only since they arrived have those crop patterns appeared!"

Tom remained silent, continuing instead, to read the coroner's report. Margaret knew, and only too well, that if it were to get out that the sheriff suspected the people up on Dugan's old farm of the brutal murders, the town's folk would most probably lay siege on them.

"You can't go speculating that they are responsible, and not without *hard* evidence!" she told the sheriff. "Just because they keep to themselves, that does not make them devil worshippers or *killers!*"

"What about *your missing* friend?" Tom asked, turning to look at her, "How well do you know *him?*" He stared at her, "It's very *odd* how he just disappeared like that!"

"I don't know what *exactly* you're suggesting, but if you think for one minute *he* did any of this, you are wrong! Very wrong!" Margaret knew Mark, and knew he couldn't, wouldn't, *kill* anyone, "He's *no* killer!"

Tom did not acknowledge her protest, but instead asked the sheriff, "What's this?" He pointed out to the sheriff, something in the coroner's report, "Traces of *Amyl Nitrate* found around the victim's mouths."

"I asked the coroner what that was, he informed me that it's used in medicines to treat heart disease. It can induce a brief euphoric state he said, and increase the heart rate and blood flow."

"Neither of my parents had heart disease!"

"Yes! That's it!" Margaret looked at Tom, "I couldn't quite put my finger on it then, but now I know what it was..!"

"What?" asked Tom, looking up from the report. "You couldn't put your finger on *what* exactly?"

"There was no *blood*!" She looked at each of them in turn, "Not a single drop!"

"How could that be sheriff?" Tom could not recall there being any either, "What did the coroner say about that?"

"He doesn't know exactly how it was done, although he did say that surgical instruments had been used and to remove body parts from the victims." He looked at Tom, then lowered his head, continuing, "He said they were alive when it had been carried out."

"So, somehow the murderer prevented any blood from leaving their bodies while removing.."

"No." Tom stopped her, "That's *not* what the sheriff meant!" Tom glared at the sheriff, "They were alive when they were being *drained* of their blood!"

The sheriff kept his gaze fixed on the floor, unable to look at Tom.

Margaret asked, "Is that right sheriff?"

"Yes, that's right," he answered, and raised his head to look at Tom, "I'm real sorry.."

"I've heard enough!" Tom slammed the file down on the sheriff's desk, "When will their bodies be released?"

"This afternoon," the sheriff replied, startled by the sudden noise.

"I've got a funeral to arrange, and *you* sheriff have a *murderer* to catch!"

"Please let me know about the funeral arrangements. I didn't know your parents well, but I know they were good, kind people," said Margaret.

"Don't you have a *friend* to find?"

"Look, he couldn't have done this! He's not.."

"He should be first on your list of suspects!" Tom told the sheriff, "For one thing *he* was the last person to see them alive!" Tom left the sheriff's office.

"Really sheriff, I've known him since.."

"That maybe so, but like Tom said, he *was* the last person to see them alive."

"Yes, I agree, but that doesn't mean *he* killed them!"

"As soon as you hear from him, you let me know. You know the penalty for obstructing the law!"

"I have no intention of obstructing justice sheriff!" Margaret had no liking for him, "But I don't think it *fair dealing* to put the blame on someone *just* because they are different or *missing*!"

"Just doing my job, young lady." He ignored her opinion, "When we find him, he will be brought in for questioning."

"Unless you want angry mobs attacking those people up on that farm sheriff, I suggest you don't go saying you think they are *devil worshippers*!"

"Don't tell me my.."

"*Job*! I know the line sheriff!" Margaret was highly-spirited and didn't take too well to being spoken down to because she was a woman. "Do that, and there will be a lot more killing done around here! And to many *more* innocent people, just like the Myers!" She didn't wait for the sheriff to reply before leaving his office. His voice alone *now* irritated her.

Chapter 8

Margaret sat at her desk incensed at the sheriff's mindset. His bigoted attitude would get people killed! The telephone rang. It was Mark! "Mark! Oh my god! Are you alright? Where are you?"

"Yes of course I'm alright. Why?"

"Where did you go off to?"

"I have something to tell you.."

Margaret interrupted him, "Harriett and Frank are dead!"

"Dead? How?"

"They were murdered!"

"What? When?"

"Some time yesterday afternoon," she told him. "You have to come back, the sheriff will need to speak to you."

"Harriett and Frank, that's terrible! Have they caught who done it?"

"No! That's why you have to come back!" she told him. "Now! As soon as possible!"

"I'm in the desert."

What was he doing in the desert? "What in the hell *for*?"

"I followed the directions given in the wheat patterns."

"What are you talking about Mark?"

"My friend Mel translated those other symbols, and found that they were directions. So I followed them!"

"To where?"

"I'm out here in the desert. There is some sort of marker I need to find.."

Margaret interrupted him, "No Mark, you need to get back here *now*!"

"I'll be back soon. That's so terrible about Harriett and Frank.."

"Until you do, the sheriff is treating you as a suspect!"

"Me! But why?"

"You were the last to see them alive!"

"No I wasn't! Whoever murdered them was!"

"Tom is home too." Margaret told him, "Come back now and when you have spoken to the sheriff, I will go with you to the desert."

"Tom? Their son? I thought he was in Vietnam."

"Yes their son. He's home!" Margaret urged, "Please Mark come back now!"

"I'll be back soon. Then I will talk to the sheriff.."

"He already suspects you had something to do with the murders, even Tom does!"

"I left the Myer's to go to Mel's to pick up the translations yesterday, straight after breakfast, and they were very much alive when I left!"

"What you're looking for in the desert can wait, just come back *now*!"

Mark replied, "Go to Mel's, he'll tell the sheriff I was at his place."

"If you don't come back, it will look very suspicious, and believe me, *this* sheriff has no problem claiming you to be guilty of their murders!"

"I really have to go now Margaret, I need to find the marker before dark."

"Mark wait!" He hung up, "Mark!" It was no use, he was gone.

Her boss walked into her office, "Are you okay?" he asked her. "What did the sheriff say about the Myer's murders?"

Margaret stared at the telephone, "He has plenty of suspects!"

"Yes, he does like to put blame before evidence that one!"

Margaret asked him, "The people that bought the Dugan's farm, have you ever met any of them?"

"A few, they keep very much to themselves though."

"What are they like?"

He sat opposite her, on the side of her desk, "Why, does the sheriff think *they* might be responsible for the killings?"

Not wanting to start any rumors in town, "No, not at all.."

He interrupted, "I bet they were the *first* on his list of suspects!"

"Well.."

"Look, all the townsfolk know what he's like; he's not what you would call; well lets just say he's a little *blinkered*."

"Bigoted!" Margaret answered.

He laughed, "You don't hold back do you!"

"Like to say how it is, that's all," she told him.

"Have you found your missing friend yet?"

"No, not yet," she lied.

"Oh I see, that wasn't him you were talking to just now then?" He got up from her desk, "You like to say how it is eh?" he winked at her. He must have heard her on the telephone to Mark.

"Oh, good story yesterday! Keep up the good work!" He left her office.

Mark, she must find him, and bring him back to speak with the sheriff, and as soon as possible. *Mel*, Mark's friend, she would go and see him, find out just *where* in the desert Mark has gone, and go after him!

Chapter 9

So many stories relating to the existence of aliens permeated society and especially so, since the story broke of a crash out in the desert. The tale of a recovered extraterrestrial craft, and its occupants, was widely talked about. Now Bram was sat opposite an alien from outer space! Bram's love of science fiction made him a keen follower of TV shows such as the *Twilight Zone* and *Voyage to the bottom of the Sea*. Also having read many books on *WW11*, and the countless reports from Airmen encountering strange craft. Government denials, cover-ups and conspiracy theories were rampant, as was reports of radar operators observing high-speed craft, superior to anything on Earth. The Air Force had known the truth, and had been covering it up all along!

"They reach our planet at different times in our history. Depending on what point in space they began their journey to Earth," the man to the beings left, told the Colonel.

"Not from one particular solar system, but travelers: *Galactic* travelers."

The being was communicating using his *mind*! The man picking up its thoughts must be some kind of *psychic*! So even using psychics was endorsed by Air Force! Bram wondered how long the government had known of the existence of aliens.

"We have always known, since the beginning of time," said the man Bram believed to be a psychic. "They have come, sometimes during events of great human conflict and upheaval."

"That is not what I asked him!" the Colonel bellowed at the psychic. "We already know all this!"

"He's answering the lieutenant Sir," the psychic told the Colonel.

"What?" The Colonel looked at Bram, "I told you to *clear* your mind!"

"Sorry Sir," Bram felt embarrassed. Everyone around the table regarded him with disapproval.

"Ask the question again!" the Colonel ordered.

The psychic continued, "Their crafts are constructed using..." He went on to give mathematical calculations. Bram began writing them down. Nothing he took down made any sense to him.

"You getting all of that lieutenant?" asked the Colonel.

"Yes Sir." Bram suspected a mathematical genius would be required to decipher any of what the being was relating to them.

An hour into the interview, and the being was clearly becoming extremely distressed. The psychic was no longer receiving any coherent messages, "I'm not getting anything from him Sir." he looked at the Colonel, "He's requesting medical assistance."

"Get them in here!" The Colonel instructed everyone around the table, "let's call it a day gentlemen."

He rose from the table and gestured to Bram to do the same, "Follow me, Lieutenant Howard." Bram stood at the far side of the room with the Colonel.

The medical team arrived.

"I'll take that file now." The Colonel took it from Bram, "You did very well, after that initial hiccup!"

"Thank you Sir." Bram looked over at the being, now being attended to, "Will he be alright?"

"We hope so." The Colonel put his hand on Bram's shoulder, "We do take care of them, you understand? But there is only so much that we can do."

"Yes Sir, I understand." Recalling his earlier reference to *War of the Worlds*, Bram asked, "They have never meant any harm to the human race then?"

"Contrary to belief, no, they have not." The Colonel continued, "I know seeing an *alien* must have come as bit of a bombshell to you, but you *will* get used to it."

Bram took from the Colonel's statement, that he would be seeing many more of these *extraterrestrials* over the next three years.

"Yes Sir," Bram replied.

"And don't worry about all that mathematical stuff, that's not for us to worry about," the Colonel told him. "That's for the scientists to figure out!"

"Yes Sir," Bram could think of nothing else to say to the Colonel.

"Well, *rocket scientists*, to be exact" He searched Bram's face for a response. Not getting one, he added, "The *Lunar* project!"

"What's that?" Bram asked. "A project to do with the *moon*?"

He smiled at Bram, "That's right, the moon!"

Looking back at the alien, now being removed by stretcher, "They keep an outpost there." The Colonel turned back to Bram, "A base. But that's only one of many they have, and scattered throughout the universe."

Bram watched as the alien was taken away, "They do? He told you all this?"

"Yes, and others before him."

Bram looked at the Colonel, "Won't the others come looking for him?"

"No. I shouldn't think so. To them, this one could be anywhere. Lost in the vast universe of space!"

"Taking notes, will that be my only duty Sir?"

"No lieutenant. There will be other tasks, but as we have little time before our alien friend becomes *deceased*, interviewing him is priority,"

"Yes Sir."

"Sergeant!" The Colonel summoned the Sergeant that had showed Bram to the room earlier. "Take the lieutenant back to his quarters."

"Yes Sir."

"I will see you in the morning lieutenant."

Chapter 10

The following morning, Bram was informed that the interview with the being had been cancelled. The being had passed away during the night. Having not slept well again, Bram felt exhausted. His head ached too. Unable to rest throughout the day, he decided a walk might help take away the pounding in his head. It was late afternoon, and the searing desert sun, now shone less fiercely upon the parched landscape. The last two days had brought much revelations.

He walked alongside the perimeter fence, looking out at the continuing arid landscape beyond it. Dust rose up from a small area in the distance, and beyond the perimeter fence. 'How can that be?' Bram wondered. It was not windy, and besides, the dust cloud was confined to only one area, and it was moving! Bram then realised what it was; the same had occurred when he drove out to the base.

There was a vehicle out there! And it was moving quite fast too, Bram noted.

At that moment something else caught his attention, having just come into view; someone was running just ahead of the vehicle! The vehicle was giving chase! The dust made it difficult to see the vehicle, but Bram could see easily that the pursued, was a man. The man changed direction, he was now running toward the perimeter fence and *Bram*!

His pursuers followed close behind, and as the vehicle got closer, Bram was able to see it was an Air base jeep. Not wanting to be seen by the police, whom he was now sure, pursued the man, Bram laid low in a hollow near the fence. He was interested in seeing who the man was, they were chasing.

"Halt!" Bram could hear the police shout, "Or we will shoot!" Bram could hear the noise of the jeep coming to a stop, and the fact that he could, now meant, they were very close to the fence, and to *him!* Bram remained hidden. He could hear the man's heavy breathing and the sound of him colliding with the fence; no, not colliding with it, but climbing it! He looked out from his place of concealment, he wanted to warn him that the top of the fence was electrified, the man saw him. He looked right at Bram, and let go of the fence, dropping to the ground. Ducking down again, Bram heard the police shout, "Stop!" He heard the noise of a struggle. "What are you doing here? This is a *restricted area*!" They had caught him. Bram heard them put him into the jeep and drive away. He came out of his hiding place. 'The man had said nothing.' 'Why hadn't he told the police he had seen him?' Bram had no idea why, but perhaps he may later, when in custody in the base's holding compound! Bram assumed that was where he would be taken and questioned. 'Who was he?' Bram wondered. 'And what was he doing out here?' He would wait until dark to find out more about the captured man.

Under cover of darkness, Bram decided to take a better look around the base, and to try to find out who the now detained man was. Ever aware of the hourly patrols, Bram used the shadows to his advantage. The base was not very well lit, for obvious reasons, the main one being, the Air Force wanted to keep the base as inconspicuous to the public as possible.

Now outside the holding compound, Bram saw the jeep used in the chase, parked outside the door. 'They must still be in there, most probably questioning the prisoner,' he thought. With no windows, he would not be able to see what was going on inside. Bram checked the door, it was open. He checked the locks on the door. 'They wouldn't be a problem to open,' he thought, and decided to return later in the night when the prisoner was alone.

Someone, moved in the shadows outside his building. Whoever it was, had seen him returning, and had quickly hid, but not quick enough! Bram knew there was no point trying to hide himself now, and stepped into the middle of the street, so as not to look suspicious. He walked to the door of his building, pretending not to see her hiding in the darkness.

Once inside, Bram hurried to one of the windows in the hallway, opened it, and slipped through. He crept along the side of the building, to where he had seen her hiding. She was still there! He moved quietly toward her. She was looking in the opposite direction, and at the door of his building. He had hoped that she would! Just as he reached her, he stretched his arm around and in front of her face. As she reacted, he quickly covered her mouth with his hand, not wanting to create a commotion, and held her tightly.

"Who are you? What are you doing here?" She struggled, unable to answer as his hand covered her mouth. "I'm not going to harm you!" She continued to struggle, tearing at his hands with her fingernails.

"I'm going to bring you inside, and then I will let you go," he told her.

Once inside but still holding on to her, "The Air police patrol the base throughout the night, if you scream they will hear you!"

Bram told her, "They will not be too happy about you being on the base! I will not harm you!" Bram promised. "Okay?"

She stopped struggling and nodded that she believed him. He let go of her.

Bram asked, "How did you get passed the police?"

She began to tie her hair up, after it had come loose in the struggle, "I'm looking for my friend."

"Is he an Airman on the base?"

"No, he is not, but I know he came here, or that he was coming here.."

Bram interrupted, "Would you like to sit down?" He indicated toward the green sofa, "It doesn't look very pretty, but it's comfortable."

"Okay, thank you," she replied, attempting a smile.

Bram sat next to, but not close, to her on the sofa, "You can trust me. I promise you no harm will come to you."

"My friend came here, he was looking for something he had seen." She stopped when she seen the headlights of a vehicle outside, "You told them I was here!" she jumped up from the sofa.

"No, I didn't! That's the Air police, they patrol the base at night!"

"Really?"

"Yes, really. Please come and sit down. I will make us some coffee. Would you like one?" Bram got up and went to the kitchen. He didn't think she would try to run away, especially with the police now patrolling the street outside.

"What is your name?" she followed him to the kitchen. "Wow! That's bad!"

Bram looked at her, he then realized she was referring to the kitchen's colour scheme.

"Yes, it's pretty bad alright!" He couldn't help noticing how very beautiful she was, "Bram Howard."

"What?"

"You asked me what my name was, *lieutenant* Bram Howard."

"Oh, yes I did." She put out her hand, "Margaret Baker."

He shook her hand, "Nice to meet you Miss Baker."

She looked back down the hallway, "You the only one here?"

"Yes, I only arrived on the base two days ago. My first posting since graduating from the Air Force academy." He handed her a mug of coffee, "Only got mugs I'm afraid."

"Green ones!" she answered.

"Yes *green*." Bram could sense she was feeling more relaxed. They both went back to the sitting room and sat down.

"Well Miss Baker, you know why I'm here, now, *why* are you here?"

"My friend telephoned me, said he was out here looking for something. I decided to come and find him."

Bram wondered if the detainee on the base was the friend she was looking for, "What is your friend's name?"

"Mark Holston." She sipped the coffee, "Two people were murdered yesterday.."

"Your friend is responsible?" asked Bram.

"Oh no, no, but he needs to speak to the sheriff, that's all."

"But he's a suspect?" Bram inquired.

"Everybody is a suspect to *that* sheriff!"

Bram didn't want to mention the captured man now being held in the base's prison, for fear she might attempt to free him.

"There is a spare room down the hall, I will sleep in there tonight, and you can have my room."

She put her coffee down on the table, "But I have to find him!"

"There's nothing you can do tonight! Get some rest, and in the morning, I will help you," Bram assured her.

"You will?"

"Yes, I promise!"

He showed her to the room she would be sleeping in, "I'll see you in the morning. Do not go outside, or you may be seen."

"Alright, I won't. Goodnight," she closed the bedroom door.

Bram sat up all night, unable to sleep, wondering how he was going to get her off the base without being seen! *Mark*, her friend, he must be the man he had seen being apprehended by the base police.

Chapter 11

"Whatever the explanation, make it an official position!" said Colonel Maxwell.

The lieutenant nodded, gathered up the papers and returned them to the file, "Weather balloon?"

"Weather balloons, light phenomena, whatever! Oh and check out that witness's background, find something; history of mental illness, any crimes committed in the past, *something*! Get it leaked to the public, by the usual means, you know the drill, discredit the eye witness, it always works. He's just another pissant anyway!" the Colonel laughed and added, "Putting doubt in peoples' minds is one approach proven to work every time!"

The lieutenant nodded in agreement, "Yes Sir, everyone's got something they don't want made public, that's their weakness."

The Colonel replied, *"Achilles heel."*

The lieutenant smiled at the Colonel's analysis, "A weather balloon incident will be set up close to the vicinity where that witness saw the craft. Our witness can be trusted to give a similar account, with a little persuasion, he's a church goer, real religious."

"Good, have him speak to the media only after your guy has spoken to him first, and be sure he understands the consequences of suggesting there are aliens visiting us!"

The lieutenant replied, "That won't be a problem, he's a non-believer for sure!"

"As long as he does exactly what we've predicted."

"He will. Any explanation for what he's seen, other than extraterrestrial, will be agreeable to *this* particular witness. He'll protect his blind faith in his god!"

The Colonel rose from his desk and walked to the window, "A religious man of good standing in the community, most reliable, and his accounts will be more credible."

"What about those murders?"

The Colonel looked out across the desert, "Hmm, not sure yet. Seems our man on the ground has been stirring up some wild accusations."

The lieutenant stood by the Colonel, "Should we leave it for the moment and see what happens?"

"We might need to implement tactic three on this one."

The lieutenant looked at the Colonel, "A disinformation campaign," he discerned,

"Cause enough chaos and any investigation will be brought to a stand still." The Colonel returned to his desk, "Precisely. How is Howard getting along?"

The lieutenant followed the Colonel, "He's a cool one."

The Colonel laughed, "Yes, not much of a reaction from him when he met with our alien friend."

"You think he was already prepared then?"

"No, I don't think so, he asked the grey the usual questions you'd expect. Could be confusing his coolness for astonishment. He was certainly rendered speechless." The Colonel added, and with a more serious tone, "Still, got to be sure, keep a close eye on him."

The lieutenant asked, "What will be his next assignment?"

"The propulsion test area and the interceptor crafts."

The lieutenant was surprised by this, "Can he be trusted?"

"Put a gun to his head, see how he reacts," the Colonel laughed.

The lieutenant however, knew it was no joke, "Wonder if he will remain so *cool* then!"

The Colonel told him, "Just give him our customary initiation!"

Chapter 12

Bram was awoken from his sleep by the same bad dream. The dream had become more frequent of late, nevertheless the outcome always remained unchanged. It begins with his quest to find and crush his old adversary. He trains his mind and body in preparation for the encounter, only to be defeated when he finally does confront his antagonist. This recurring outcome frustrates Bram, leaving him emotionally weary.

Now fully awake, Bram could hear that Margaret was already up. Still dressed from the night before, having laid on top of the covers, not wanting to be horribly itched all night by the unpleasant wire-like material of the military blankets, he found her in the kitchen, "How did you sleep?"

She seemed startled, "Not at all."

Surprised by her answer, as he had given her his most treasured possessions; his feather down duvet and pillows, "Oh, was the bed not comfortable?"

"The bed was just fine, I'm just so worried about my friend."

Relieved to hear that the bed had not been the problem, "Of course."

"Would you like some coffee? I've just made a pot."

"Yes thank you," Bram couldn't help but stare, she was very pretty, but not the pretty found in a fashion magazine, there was a genuine beauty in her, he thought. Nothing superficial or staged, but an attractiveness that shone through without the need for makeup and designer clothes. Her green eyes were as captivating as her soft voice, and he supposed she never had need to raise it to be heard.

"I couldn't find anything else in.."

Bram interrupted her, "I'm not hungry, the coffee will be fine thanks."

"Sorry, I don't mean to be bad-mannered, by helping myself, I just need to keep busy.."

Again Bram stopped her, "It's okay, I understand. Make yourself at home."

"Thank you."

"But it's not safe for you here, and we need to get you off this base before someone sees you."

"I don't want to get you in any trouble."

"You can't do it on your own," Bram told her.

"I got here on my own!"

"Yes how did you..?"

It was Margaret's turn to interrupt, "It's not important right now, but finding my friend is."

Bram suggested they talk further in the living room. Margaret brought the coffee pot.

"I'll pick up something for you from the base canteen, you have to eat, coffee will not be enough to keep you going."

"Thank you. You're very kind."

Bram now feeling a little embarrassed, replied "You don't know me yet!"

Margaret looked at him, smiled but said nothing.

"Why don't you tell me from the beginning, what brought you and your friend out here," Bram felt awkward by her silence.

"Well okay." Margaret put her now empty coffee cup on the table.

Bram couldn't help his mind from wandering, her indisputable pure beauty captivated him. She was a journalist, just recently graduated from college, and working on her first story with a small time newspaper, that much he learned, but he wanted to know the real Margaret, but he knew that was unlikely to happen. He had his duty at the base to fulfil.

"The crop formations started to appear about a week ago.."

"Crop formations?"

Margaret explained, "Yes, patterns constructed out of the wheat growing in the fields."

"Do these patterns mean something?"

"Well that's what my friend Mark was trying to discover. He sketched down some and took them to a friend who had studied cryptology, to see if he could decipher their meaning, if they had any.."

"And did they indicate anything?"

"Yes, one implied that a conduit was coming! Supposedly meaning information given in secret, or secret information, well something like that."

Bram replied, "Supervillian."

"What?"

"Conduit could also mean supervillian, the supervillian is coming!"

"Like a powerful enemy or foe?"

Bram answered, "Yes, a powerful adversary of some kind."

"That is maybe, but my friend is now missing because of me!"

Bram took her hand, "I promise to help you find him." Bram already had his suspicions that the man held on the base was her friend. He was surprised by his easy willingness to help her, as he knew only too well it would not be easy.

"Thank you," she told him.

"What happened then?"

"Mark decided to camp out all night on the Myer's farm, to see if he could discover who or what was responsible for creating the patterns."

"And did he?"

"No, but he did determine that no human had been responsible."

"No human., machine?"

"Yes, although of what kind, he did not know."

"How is it you came looking for him out here, in the desert?"

Bram noticed the change in her demeanour, she seemed uncomfortable by his question, "Are you alright?"

"Yes., yes it's just.."

Bram tried to assure her that she did not have to tell him everything straight away, "It's okay, take your time, we can continue with this later.."

"No, I'm fine, really, but you need to know everything, if you are to help me. My story was published the next morning." she continued. "I waited at the newspaper office all day but heard nothing from Mark or the Myer's. Then at 5pm I went out to the farm to find Mark. He was not at his camp site so I went up to the farmhouse. You see he's very likable, and Mrs Myer had began to grow quite fond of him, even cooked him meals all the time he was camped out on their farm."

Bram became aware that her beautiful green eyes had welled up with tears, "Are you sure you're okay to continue?"

"Yes, I'm fine."

Bram watched her wipe away a tear before it had the chance to trickle down her face. "Would you like some more coffee," he gestured to the pot she had brought from the kitchen.

"Thank you," she nodded.

Bram filled her coffee cup and passed it to her.

"When I reached the farmhouse I noticed right away that all was not right. The screen door, along with the front door, had been pulled or ripped off their hinges."

Bram looked at her, but said nothing.

She cradled the coffee cup in her hands, "I called out but no one answered. When I.. oh god., what I saw.." Margaret's hands began to shake, and pretty soon she was trembling all over.

Bram held her hands to steady them, afraid the hot coffee would spill out, burning her.

"They had been murdered: brutally murdered!"

Bram took the coffee cup from her hands, "You've obviously had a traumatic experience, maybe we should leave this conversation.."

Margaret rose to her feet, and began pacing nervously, "No, I want to continue. Now all that's important is finding Mark, and soon, before he's charged with their murders!"

Bram got to his feet, "He murdered them?"

"Oh no., Not Mark. He never harmed anyone in his life. It's that sheriff, the intolerable fool. He even believes devil worshippers maybe responsible!"

"I see," replied Bram, but he didn't see, he was quite confused. "You said that you found them murdered, what made you think they had been murdered?"

Margaret stopped pacing and turned to look at him, "Their bodies, they had been mutilated!"

"In what way do you mean?"

She began pacing the room again, "I've never seen anything like it. Their eyes, tongues and internal organs had all been removed!"

Bram was taken aback by what she was telling him, nevertheless, he couldn't help thinking he had heard of this before. The mutilations of the naive farmer and his wife had a strange familiarity to them. Then it hit him, "That's it., that's where I heard of that before!"

Margaret looked at him, surprised at his outburst, "Heard of what?"

"Not too long ago out in Texas, some farmers reported their cattle being killed and mutilated. Their eyes, tongues and sex organs were always missing when the farmers had found the animals."

"Really? Did they discover who had done it?"

"Not who, but what had done it. Or at least what they believed to be the only reasonable explanation; wild dogs, they said."

Margaret answered, "Look no dogs could have done to the Myers what I saw!"

Bram agreed, "No, most likely not, and probably not to those poor dumb animals in Texas either!"

"Who then? Do you think they are connected? Some kind of deranged killer, having slaughtered animals as practise, and only moving on to people when his method of killing had been finely tuned?"

Bram answered, although almost to a whisper, "Nothing of this world."

Margaret still heard him, "What do you mean?"

Bram regretted saying this the moment he heard himself say it, and changing the subject, he asked, "But why do you think he's out here in the desert?"

"The patterns also revealed a map, with directions that led to this base."

Bram was now even more curious as to why directions to a top secret air base should be encrypted into flattened down wheat, "That is very strange as this base doesn't even show up on any map!"

"Well here I am!"

Bram looked at her in puzzlement, "Yes, here you are," and continued, "Whatever is going on with these wheat patterns, I have no idea, but what is important right now is finding your friend, and getting you both out of here, and I think I know where he is."

"You do?"

"Describe him to me."

Chapter 13

"All we need, is someone like that person who caused an uproar about a certain chemical being used, and with a little *anonymous* backing, the government will be forced to ban the offending chemical, then just sit back and let the deaths mount up!"

"That's one way I guess."

"But that's *one way* we've used before!"

The dimly lit room stank of stale cigar smoke. Five men in their tailor-made suits, sat around the large oval, oak table. One of them spoke to the others, "I'm afraid one of our members has had a heart attack and now remains in a coma, but we shall continue as normal."

"As we left off on our last meeting gentlemen," said another, "I was saying then, look at how many people die of malaria each year. Nearly a million last year," he continued. The others all shook their heads in agreement. "3.3billion people, half the worlds population are at risk of malaria. So to loose half the worlds population when the time comes, would certainly be feasible!" There was an agreeable muttering from the men gathered round the table. "Just keep things as they are, minimal intervention, then when *that time* comes, all intervention will cease and nature will take its course!

In the meantime if someone develops., say a chemical that works, then we assist in getting it banned," he added.

"Or buy all rights to it!" The man next to him stated.

"Exactly," he replied.

Each joined the conversation whenever they had something to add. No one man in the room was in charge, they were all equal in status; all as powerful as each other.

"Only certain diseases are in our best interest to control, ones that affect the rich developed countries."

Another spoke, "You mean countries that we and our families live in!" The room reverberated from the sound of the men's laughter.

"That goes without saying!" replied another.

"Keeping our people free of disease, keeps us free of disease!"

Three of the men answered in unison, "We know this!"

The sound of low muttering filled the room, as each discussed their individual issues with the man next to him.

Then one spoke up to address all of them, "We have more than world population control to discuss." They all looked at him in disapproval. Seeing this he added, "That is always top of our agenda of course." They nodded their agreement with the latter statement and he continued, "The crop failures predicted, have resulted in the current condition of the markets, as also foreseen. Now is the time to put into action the next step. The same procedure as many times before of course, however we could go a little further with it this time, considering the current economic climate globally."

They all nodded in agreement. "I suggest, and like we've done before, a little more chaos in the market of the country we specified in our last meeting. It is time to move excess population from that said country. Are we all in agreement?" He looked round the table, for the men's approval.

"The responsibility for recessions, resulting migrations and emigrations, are always put on governments, and this time will be no different!"

Another of the men spoke out, "Governments come and go, ultimately we, and our descendants will continue to maintain our existence at the top!"

"Greedy men make greedy governments!" said another.

"Here, here!" they all replied.

"The nicest, kindest man or woman, with all the best intentions in the world, soon becomes overwhelmed by the desire for power. Becoming greedy and disloyal to their people. The very same people they promised to serve. Every decision thereafter, is made with their own personal desires in mind!"

Another of the men added, "A favor here and there to persons that can further theirs, or their loved ones' careers!"

Each of the men had an opinion to add. "Giving them the leg-up they otherwise would never have gotten!"

"The human condition!" said another. "There is no wealth or power more or greater than all we possess. We are the only ones that can be trusted!"

"Let's get on with it gentlemen."

"What about our absent honorable member?"

"We cast a vote without him, as he remains ill."

Chapter 14

Bram had gotten to his feet the moment he had heard the sound of the approaching Jeep, "Go back to the bedroom. Stay there until I tell you otherwise." He ushered Margaret down the corridor to the bedroom, "Just stay in here and please don't make a sound."

"What is it?"

"We've got company."

"Who?"

Bram looked toward the living room window and saw the lieutenant getting out of the Jeep, he was now walking toward the door, "No time to explain, go!"

Margaret did as he said.

Bram returned to the living room and before the lieutenant could knock, Bram opened the door, "Oh I'm just on my way to the canteen, I'm starving!"

The startled lieutenant replied, "That's why I'm here, I am to take you there."

"Great, let's go," Bram closed the door behind him and followed the lieutenant to the jeep, looking at his wristwatch to check the time, "You're a little early."

The lieutenant started up the engine and pulled away, "I've to take you to a briefing first, then I'll drop you off at the canteen."

"Isn't the briefing hall next to the canteen?"

"Yes it is, but we are not going there."

The lieutenant turned the jeep into the direction of the base runway.

"Oh right, the briefing will be at flight command?"

The lieutenant did not answer, just swung the jeep round and pulled up outside the base holding compound.

Bram looked at the building and then at the lieutenant, "Here? Why here?"

"This is where you will be briefed. All will be explained in a moment," the lieutenant told him, and pointed to two waiting armed, base police officers. "They will show you where to go from here," he told Bram, as he reached across him opening Bram's door.

"I will wait here for you and take you to the canteen after you've been briefed."

Bram stepped out of the jeep and walked toward the two officers.

Had he been seen at the compound the night before? And had they followed him back to his quarters only to find that he had a civilian, a woman, on the base? Bram tried to remain calm, continuing to walk toward the waiting police. Inside he wanted to run, and in the opposite direction, but he would have no chance, they were armed and would not hesitate in shooting him in the back as he tried to get away.

"This way," said one of the officers, his hands firmly gripping his weapon.

Bram entered the compound his heart pounding hard against his ribs, "Why here?"

The same officer answered, "Briefing on your next assignment." The other remained silent.

Bram was *sure* he was being lured into a waiting cell, the officers not wanting to make a fuss until they had him securely locked behind bars. Then all would be revealed; he had been seen the night before!

The compound had no windows, as Bram already knew from the previous night's visit. Florescent tube lighting provided the only light to the grey concrete walls and floors. Bram walked along the corridor, flanked either side by the two officers. All the heavy metal cell doors were open wide, and as Bram passed each one he checked for Margaret's missing friend. *Margaret!* What were they doing to her? They must have her by now? Having waited until he was gone to break in and capture her! There would be nothing he could do to help her now, *hell.,* he couldn't even help himself now!

At the end of the corridor, and leading to the back of the compound Bram guessed, was an even larger metal door, the sign above it read-'*Disciplinary* Station.'

Bram was in no doubt now that he had been found out. One of the officers stepped in front of Bram to open the door, while the other stood behind Bram ordering him to enter the room.

"What is this all about?" Bram asked, even though he knew exactly why he had been brought here; to be interrogated!

One chair, placed in the centre of the room, faced the door. There was nothing else in that dim, windowless room.

"Take a seat."

Bram reluctantly sat down. The interrogation would soon begin. He had already decided to tell all before entering the compound, to ensure Margaret would not have to suffer at the hands of trained interrogators. Bram knew only too well that after telling them everything they wanted to know, Margaret would be questioned. She would confirm all he had said, and she would then not be harmed.

"We are responsible for the security of this base," said one of the officers, the other continuing to remain silent.

"Yes, I am aware of that," Bram wanted to be as compliant as possible under the circumstances.

The officer told him, "What goes on at this base is never to be revealed beyond its perimeters."

Bram looked at them both in turn, nodding that he understood.

Taking a hand pistol from his holster, the silent officer pointed it at Bram.

Bram yelled out, "What is this? What have I done?"

"Nothing!"

Bram was not expecting that answer, "Nothing?"

The officer looked at him curiously, "Why, is there something you want to tell us?"

Bram wondered if this was all part of their interrogation technique, and was unsure of what to answer.

"Well is there?"

Bram took a chance, "No! Of course not!"

The officer placed the pistol to Bram's left temple. Bram swallowed hard. He had given his answer. He must hold out; stand by his answer. "I have nothing to tell you!"

"Are you sure about that?"

The other officer pressed the pistol hard against his head.

"There is nothing!" Bram shouted out.

"Well that's okay then."

The officer removed the pistol from Bram's head, but kept it pointed at him.

"Just as long as you understand the consequences."

Bram, still confused, even now was not sure if they knew anything or not, "Is this my briefing?"

They looked at one another and laughed at his question. That was the first time Bram had heard a sound out of the reticent officer.

"Is it?" Bram asked again.

"I guess you could say it is," they both continued laughing.

"Are we finished then?"

The laughter stopped, "Yes! We are finished with you, for now." The officer returned the pistol to his holster.

"We'll walk you out."

Bram considered that if he had a weapon, and along with the strong desire he felt right at that moment, he could easily have killed them both without any hesitation. Now out of the compound, he joined the lieutenant in the jeep. The lieutenant did not speak to Bram until dropping him off at the canteen.

"You will have to walk back to your quarters from here when you're done. I'll pick you up from there at noon. Enjoy your breakfast." Bram was in no humour to answer.

The canteen was empty all except for two canteen staff behind the counter and technical Sergeant Elliot Dayton, who was sat alone. He looked up at Bram but said nothing. Bram went to the counter and took what he needed.

"Are you eating here Sir or taking out?" asked one of the kitchen staff.

"Both."

"I see, what would you like Sir?"

"The full breakfast," Bram planned on sitting next to Dayton, "I'll be over there."

"Okay Sir, I'll bring it over in a moment."

"Thank you," Bram walked over and sat down at the same table as Dayton,

"Morning."

Dayton looked at him enquiringly, "Good morning," he answered.

"Yes, a very good morning, in fact the kind of morning you'd like nothing better than to have a gun put to your head!"

"What?"

Bram laughed at Dayton's bewilderment, "Oh nothing, just a private joke," he told him.

"Right.." answered Dayton still looking at Bram warily.

Bram was still reeling at having a gun put to his head. Adrenalin still at a high in his body from the experience, "I know we are not to talk of our assignments to one another but., I tell you," Bram smiled and shook his head, "what is going on here is very strange, very strange indeed!"

Dayton grabbed hold of Bram's arm, "Look, I don't want any trouble, so why don't you go and sit somewhere else?"

Bram pulled his arm away, "Fine, but it will happen to you too!"

"Just go away!"

"I'm going! But before I do, you haven't seen a civilian round here have you? A man, unshaven, hippie clothes.."

"No I haven't."

"Well if you do.."

"Just go away," Dayton told him.

"Just asking a question," Bram went to another table, pulled out a chair and slammed it to the floor. The two kitchen staff looked over at him, one called out to him, "Is everything alright Sir?"

Bram looked at them and then at Dayton, "Yes, just dandy!"

After breakfast was brought to his table, Bram sat silently playing with the food on the plate. He was in no mood to eat. Getting up from his seat, he approached the counter and asked for a container to take the breakfast back to his quarters. Bram looked over in the direction of Dayton, "I don't like the company in here!" he declared. The kitchen staff looked at Bram curiously. Dayton paid no attention to the remark and carried on eating. Taking the container of food, Bram made his way back to his quarters, and to Margaret. Anger welled up inside him, it surprised him at how having a gun put to his head, could make him feel this way. He just couldn't shake the rage he felt.

Chapter 15

After hearing the front door close, and the jeep pull away from the building, only then did Margaret leave her hiding place to find Bram gone. She had not been able to make out clearly what the conversation had been about, however, she had heard Bram say, he was starving, and figured he was gone to the base's canteen in the jeep. Her stomach made a grumbling noise, she was hungry too. Not surprising her stomach moaned in protest; she hadn't eaten for almost twenty four hours! Nothing for it, at least until Bram returned, but to drink more coffee.

Margaret sat in silence on the sofa, holding the coffee cup in both hands. The stillness all around had a calming affect on her. Putting down the coffee cup, she lay back on the sofa, and stared up at the low ceiling. A feeling of serenity began to wash over her, and this surprised her. With all that had occurred in the last week, how could it be possible to feel so as peace? She struggled to protest against it, but was unable to stop herself from drifting further into a state of total quiet. She attempted to lift her arms, but found she was unable to. Her whole body felt suddenly anaesthetized.

Then it struck her, perhaps it was the coffee! Had Bram put something in it when she wasn't looking? After all he had encouraged her to drink more, and had even filled her cup! She was unable to panic. The feeling of it was there, but it was unable to come forward, held back by the overwhelming desire to be at peace. She may very well have misjudged him, he was not going to help her after all! Most likely leaving when he did to give the drug a chance to do it's job. Then return when she was completely helpless to do anything; unconscious and unaware.

The harder she tried the stronger the feeling of calm washed over her. In all her life, she could never have thought, that the serenity she was now experiencing, would be so unwelcome. Most people hope and wish to feel this way, even spending a lot of time and money on all sorts of ways to calm body and soul. Margaret then realised something, she was fully aware of how she was feeling! Her mind did not feel hazy or drunk, as it should, if she had been drugged. Although her body was sedated, her mind was not!

Someone spoke. Margaret heard somebody speak. The gentle, serene voice came again. Margaret heard it, but not with her ears, her mind! Unable to make any sense of what was being said, Margaret listened. It was as though she were only hearing one side of a conversation. There were answers without questions, and questions without answers. That was the only way she could describe it. Then she heard another voice, quiet at first, but now becoming louder, as if the person speaking was moving closer to her. Now she could hear both sides of the conversation.

They are not talking to her, although they are aware of her, and they want her to hear them; they want their communications to be intercepted. They are *aliens!* She knew this because they told her, and she can feel it too. They are not the same as her or any other human. They allow her to look into their very souls, their souls more apparent than their organic bodies. This is how they are to one another. They look into each other's souls like people look into one another's eyes when they first meet. Their soul or spirit, as Margaret understood, was the important thing, the body only a vessel for it. A vessel to be respected and cared for, as it performs such an valuable function.

Margaret knew no drug was responsible for what she was experiencing, it was real! They knew all about the crop formations, although they did not own up to being responsible for creating them. Margaret then remembered what Bram had said about the mutilations; *nothing of this world.* She asked, although not in words but in thought, if they or their kind had been responsible for the brutal murders of the Myers. She got the feeling they objected to being asked this question. Margaret could sense they meant no harm to the human race. They do not however, like our world leaders.

Margaret feels confused by their idea of world leaders. They don't refer to world leaders as presidents or governments, but by something else. She does not understand what they are conveying to her, as the concept of such a leadership would be unimaginable. They feel her confusion and tell her that is how it is. And although she can not perceive such a leadership, it nonetheless exists! The world's leaders do not belong to one country, but all countries. They do not have alligence to one nation, as people do, such as people from America see themselves as Americans and so on, these leaders, as shown to her, see themselves as earth people only.

The aliens show even lower contempt for the people Margaret does understand to be world leaders; governments, regimes, administrative establishments. They see them as being greedy, egotistic, with insatiable appetites for power and control. They tell Margaret these leaders are more organic than soul, more flesh than spirit, only seeking to fulfil the needs of the flesh and so can not be trusted. She understands but is unable to comprehend fully. She does sense also, that they feel some pity toward those who relentlessly strive for fulfilment of the flesh, as they see it to be an impossible goal, and believe them to be foolishly materialistic, idealistic, and some, even *insane*.

Nevertheless, they have not given up on the human race altogether, she feels, and they believe not everyone is beyond redemption. In fact, there are many people already on the right course to salvation. Margaret senses from them, that something is coming. They can not hold it back for much longer; *the conduit is coming*. Margaret was taken aback, so much so that she sat bolt upright upon hearing those words. The fear, like that of her worst nightmare becoming reality, shot through her. She had no idea why those words should put such fear into her. She listened but could no longer hear them. The door opened. It was Bram returning.

Chapter 16

"He's not on the base."

Margaret, still recovering from her strange experience, asked, "Who?" But quickly realised who he meant, "Mark! You mean Mark!"

"Of course I meant Mark."

"Sorry, but something very odd just happened to me.."

Bram walked over to where she was sitting, put down the food container he was carrying, and emptied his pockets onto the table, "Yes well," he said, "something very strange happened to me also." The walk back had calmed his fury, but only a little, "Those bastards put a gun to my head!"

"Who? Who would do that?"

"The base police, and to scare me, but that don't scare me, all it makes me want to do is get a gun and shoot those two morons!"

"To scare you., but why?"

Bram realised he couldn't tell her why, "Just Air Force crap," he lied.

"I see, well if infuriating you was their aim, they certainly achieved it!"

"Yes., sorry, I really shouldn't let it bother me so much.."

Margaret interrupted, "It's fine. What's with all this?" Margaret pointed to the mound of individually wrapped doughnuts, cookies and pastries, on the table.

Bram opened the container, "Have this," he told her, "they can keep," he pointed to the pile of wrapped food on the table. "I'll get you a plate, it may need warming up though."

"Have you eaten?"

Bram answered, "No, I don't want anything for now." He went to the kitchen and switched on the oven.

His reason for joining the Air Force was all that prevented him from doing anything foolish. Bram placed the food on a tray and put it into the now warmed oven. He couldn't tell Margaret that the reason he suspected, was to make certain he understood the consequences of letting anyone know what was going on at the base. Margaret would be the worst kind to tell; she was a journalist! Although he wondered if he would ever get her off the base without being caught. Worse still, if he did get caught helping her and it was discovered she was a journalist, he suspected he would surely be shot!

"You said Mark's not here on the base, how do you know this?"

Bram turned to see Margaret standing in the doorway with the coffee pot in her hand.

"I went to the holding compound where I'd seen him being taken to, and now he's not there. All the cells were empty."

"Could he have been taken somewhere else on the base?" Margaret began making more coffee.

Bram knew that would be the only place her friend would be allowed to see, he certainly wouldn't be taken any place else, security and secrecy being as it was. "No I don't believe so." Bram figured her friend most likely, had been given the same treatment as he had received earlier, before releasing him. "Your friend must have been released sometime in the night or earlier this morning."

"Are you sure?"

"Well no, but without going up to those two and asking them outright, that is the most probable assumption."

"Yes, I suspect you're right." Margaret filled the coffee pot, "thank you helping me."

Bram looked at her, "It's fine, you don't have to thank me. What's important now is to get you safely off this base." He had been thinking of a way, however, they would have to wait until dark. Bram took out the food from the oven, "Looks okay, I think."

Margaret looked over at the tray, "Divide it onto two plates, you have to eat something," she handed Bram two plates. "If he has been released he'll go straight to my office looking for me. Oh no! The sheriff, he'll be waiting to arrest him!"

"Tonight. I will help you get off the base tonight," he assured her. "When I get back, as I have to go at noon."

"I don't want to get you into any trouble," Margaret told him.

Bram shared out the food onto the plates, "Here," Bram passed her the plates, "take these into the living room, I'll bring the coffee."

Margaret took the two plates, "Alright."

Sitting together in the living room, Bram said, "But if he had nothing to do with the murders, he hasn't got anything to be worried about."

"I know, but it's that sheriff, he'll lock him up first and ask questions later!" Margaret picked up the two coffee cups they had used earlier and began filling them with fresh coffee from the pot, "and after having being locked up here on the base too, well, it won't be very nice for him."

"No, I guess not."

She passed him the filled coffee cup, "The sooner I get back the better."

Bram checked the time on his wrist watch, "It'll be noon soon and I have something to do before that lieutenant arrives."

"What are you planning on doing?"

Bram replied, "Best you don't know," then taking a mouthful of coffee, "You make good coffee."

"Thank you."

Bram looked at her, she was so beautiful he thought, "You seemed a little disoriented when I returned earlier."

Margaret put down her coffee, "Yes that's right, what happened to me was very strange. I don't quite know how to explain it, but I over heard a conversation; an *alien* conversation!"

Bram's eyes widened, "What? Here?"

"Yes, while I was sitting here!"

"What was it you heard?"

"There was so much, and I'm not sure if I can recall"

"Where were these aliens?"

"Well, they were not here exactly, they were in my head." Margaret realised how crazy that may have sounded, "What I mean is, I could hear their conversation, in my mind!"

She continued to explain further until it struck her, why was it he hadn't seemed surprised by the mentioning of *aliens*? "You asked me what had I heard, and if they had been here, but you asked nothing of the fact that I said they were *aliens*."

Bram didn't want to tell her about the aliens on the base, dead or otherwise, "Didn't I?"

"No, you didn't!"

Bram thought it wise to follow her question with another, "Aliens? What made you believe they were aliens anyway?"

It worked Margaret continued, "They told me, no that's not right, they showed me!"

"They showed you?"

"I don't know how else to describe it, but it was all very clear in my mind what they were. And I'm not mad, I can assure you of that!"

"I don't think you're crazy," Bram told her.

"Well that's reassuring to know."

Bram smiled at her answer, knowing full well she was being cynical.

Margaret then went on to tell him what she had learned from the alien conversation, "They spoke with contempt for our world leaders, but I found it difficult to understand who they believed our world leaders to be."

Bram asked, "How so?"

"Well they're not part of any government or of any one nationality, but all nationalities!"

"This group of leaders are a mix of leaders from around the world? So they meant the United Nations? They don't like the UN?"

"No, I don't think that's what they meant at all."

"What makes you so sure?"

"They showed the group to me, explained how they operate, and I'm quite aware of what the United Nations is, and it was certainly *not* what was shown to me!"

Bram was taken aback by her protest, "Alright so it wasn't the UN, what other group then?"

"I don't know, but do you remember I told you about Mark's cryptologist friend?

And what he had said about the patterns in the wheat?"

Bram recalled, "that something or someone was coming?"

"Yes, that the conduit is coming, well that is what they told me also!"

"Are you sure you didn't just fall asleep on the sofa and dream all of this?"

Margaret was visibly irritated at his suggestion, "No! I was not asleep!"

"Sorry, I didn't mean to..."

Margaret interrupted, "Look I wasn't asleep, in fact for a moment I thought.." she stopped, realising that it would be best not to tell him how she had initially thought he had drugged her coffee.

"You thought what?"

"That I had fallen asleep," she lied.

"Well, whatever the reason for hearing alien voices, it won't help you get off this base," Bram answered, and added, "I will be back in a few minutes, what I have to do won't take long." He got to his feet and headed for the kitchen, calling back to her, "Keep a look out; let me know if anyone is coming!"

"Okay!" Margaret called to him and went to the living room window.

Chapter 17

"All's been taken care of Sir"

"How did he react?"

"Scared!"

"Not such a cool one then after all."

"No, Sir."

"You can count on our first-rate gentlemen of the Air base police to put the fear of God into the bravest man!"

"Yes Sir, I guess we can."

"Take him to the propulsion test area and make sure he is shown the interceptor crafts."

"The interceptor crafts?"

"Yes, I want him to see them."

"Yes Sir, but so soon?"

"Just do it, lieutenant!"

"Yes Colonel."

"And what was the result from the balloon incident? Did our witness' statement convey to the public all we had hoped it would?"

"Yes and more., god that guy.." the lieutenant mocked, "You sure can't make people like that!"

"He's a natural then?"

"Yes Sir., a natural moron!" They laughed contemptuously.

The Colonel still smiling asked, "Did the press get their pictures?"

"Yes Sir, made sure of it. Even managed to get a weather expert on board."

"What for?"

"Well it turned out that our natural moron," the lieutenant again mocked, "had a friend who happens to be a self-acclaimed weather expert, and he of course backed up his friend's opinion that nothing extraterrestrial was in our skies."

The Colonel asked, "What was it he said?"

"Weather conditions and cloud formations *can* and *do* play tricks on the mind."

"Brilliant!" replied the Colonel, most pleased.

"And furthermore, he informed the press that it is a fact that desert atmosphere provides an infinity of explanations, other than aliens!"

"Good, good, all went as planned. That should leave enough doubt in the public's mind about what has been seen in our skies." The Colonel sat at his desk, an open file lay open in front of him, looking at it, he told the lieutenant, "One of them is now on the base," he closed the file.

The lieutenant looked at the closed file, "For any particular reason, Sir?"

The Colonel picked up the closed file, pushed his chair back from his desk and got to his feet, "Yes., to see how our newest experiments are working out."

"But we're no way near any answers yet!"

"Relax lieutenant, they know that, but that won't stop them from wanting to take a look at the progress so far." The Colonel returned the file to the safe, "I'm informed we have a new test subject."

"Yes Sir, we do."

The Colonel sat back at his desk, "Well you better get on with it."

"Yes Sir. This is probably not the best time to bring this up Colonel, but those murders?"

"No it's not lieutenant, however you have a point, it will need sorting out."

"Had you anything in mind Sir?"

"Not as yet, but I have been giving it some thought."

"Nothing has moved on the ground so far, although our man is a little unstable at times."

The Colonel shook his head, "He's not just prejudiced then?"

"No Sir."

"Why is it they turn out to be mad too!"

"He is somewhat crazy Sir."

"Well make sure you steer him in the right direction before he looses it completely!"

"Yes Sir, but I think because he's held that position for some time, and people have now gotten to know him, that when he snaps it won't come as a shock to anyone."

"Even better, and when he does, make sure he too is the one the public point the finger at for those murders!"

"Is that how you want it set up Colonel?"

"It would seem it's the only way. We can always find another lunatic."

The lieutenant replied, "That's for sure! Will that be all Sir?"

"Yes that's all. I will join the team later, see how our new guy is getting along."

"Howard Sir?"

"Yes, Howard."

Chapter 18

Bram was now on his way to his new assignment, having left Margaret alone back at his quarters. He hadn't spoken to the lieutenant on the way to the hollowed out mountain, still fuming from what had happened to him that morning in the holding compound. The lieutenant had not said very much to Bram either, just pointed him in the right direction once inside the cave, before driving away.

Another Air base police officer, and one Bram had not met before, was waiting for him by the security entrance. "Good afternoon lieutenant Howard, if you would just follow me."

Bram didn't speak to him, only nodded in response, and followed the officer down the inclining corridor. From Bram's calculation, they were heading toward the back of the mountain. The further down they went, the wider the corridor became, until they reached a considerably sizable space. This area was much larger, considerably larger than the common area at the other side of the excavated mountain.

Bram looked around, his brain unable to register quick enough, all that his eyes were seeing. Alien craft; some new, some old and more crass than others. Craft design that bordered the ridiculous, as well as those that seemed ingenious, were lined up side by side. To the far end of the huge open area, and where light flooded in from the outside, was an entrance much greater than that on the opposite side of the mountain. Bram figured that was how the crafts had been brought into the mountain.

The Colonel approached them, "I'll take it from here, " he told the officer. "Well lieutenant, this is where you will be working from now on."

"Yes Sir."

"We will be requiring your flying skills."

Bram could still only manage to repeat, "Yes Sir."

"I bet you have many questions you would like to ask," the Colonel looked at him, waiting for a response.

"Yes, yes I have," Bram allowed his eyes to gaze upon each and every one of the crafts in turn. "Where did they come from?"

"Some are our own, and some are not."

"The greys?"

"Yes."

"Why are they all either circular or elliptical in shape?"

The Colonel seemed amused by Bram's question, "As you most probably already know, there is no atmosphere in space.."

Bram not wanting to seem foolish interrupted, "I am fully aware of that Sir."

"Quite, and as a pilot, you will also be *aware* that in order to change direction you need something to bank against, yes?"

Bram understood what the Colonel meant, "Yes, I see, so with no atmosphere there is nothing to bank the craft against in order to facilitate directional change."

"Correct! There are small engines built in, and all around the edges of the crafts. These can be individually fired. What engine is chosen, depends on what direction the craft is required to go."

"I see."

"That is not all, there is also the main engine of course and that is not as straight forward. Well at least not with our alien crafts."

Bram asked, "What do you mean?"

"You will see, but for now, there are some scientists here that will show you around.

You will be required to assist them in flying these crafts."

"Flying them? I wouldn't know how?"

"That is what you are here to learn, *how,* and when you have figured it out, you're to explain it to them."

"But, I.."

"Look lieutenant, you are the pilot, your job is to fly crafts, so fly them!"

"Yes Sir, I'll do my best Sir."

A group of men in white coats and clipboards in their hands, stood under one of the crafts. It was one of the larger crafts, silver in colour and oval in shape.

The Colonel took Bram over to them, "This is lieutenant Howard, he will be here to assist you in test flying these crafts."

Bram shook each of their hands in turn, and with the introductions over with, the Colonel left Bram with the scientists.

"What drives these crafts?"

One of the scientists' answered, "Photon propulsion."

Bram didn't pretend to know what the scientist meant, however, he also didn't feel that he'd understand any better if he asked what that was, "I see.." he answered.

The scientist looked at him, "A reaction is generated by electromagnetic radiation, that reaction is thrust," the scientist explained.

"Right, I get the idea, I don't fully understand of course."

"Of course," the scientist replied.

"How is it we have so many of these crafts, and why so many different types?"

"I don't think that's the reason you are here," answered another of the scientists.

"What do you mean?"

"You will get on a lot better if you *don't* ask questions like that," another of them told Bram. "Mass increases at the speed of light, if no mass then you would get everywhere instantly," said another of the scientists, taking the attention away from Bram. He felt he was getting deeper in over his head, and wondered if he'd made the right decision getting himself posted to the desert base. He hoped Margaret was alright back at his quarters. He would be much relieved when she was no longer on the base.

While the scientists continued their conversation, Bram was unable to take his eyes off the many types of flying disk-like crafts. They discussed gravity, propulsion, utilising solar power, and some other stuff Bram had never heard of before, except maybe in episodes of some of his favourite sci-fi programmes. How was he supposed to fly any of these other-worldly crafts? More importantly, where did they all come from?

Just then Bram saw the interceptor aircrafts, two Convair F-102's. This in itself was not unusual, as they were built as part of the Air Force's defence against Soviet Union bomber fleets. What *was* strange though, was why it was that they should be here, as all had currently been deployed for use in the Vietnam War? Whatever the reason for the presence of F-102's, with their nose-mounted infrared search and track, along with carrying the

Gar 9 nuclear falcons, very-long-range air to air missiles, Bram could not even tender a guess, nevertheless, the Air Force were now using them, and here in the desert!

Chapter 19

Bram returned to find Margaret in quite an anxious and troubled state. "I've been thinking all day, what if Mark finds out from his friend Mel, that I came to see him?" she asked him.

"Why are you so concerned about that?"

"Well don't you see? The symbols? That led here!"

"What., and you think he'll come back out here?"

"Yes., to look for me!"

Bram recalled his own experience at the hands of the Air base police, "After being here once, I shouldn't think he would want to return."

"That wouldn't matter, in fact, that would give him *more* reason to come back out here!"

"Maybe," Bram answered, not fully convinced, as Margaret was unaware of how even *he,* who was authorized to be on the base, had had a gun put to his head.

"I've got to get back right away!"

"Look, until nightfall there is no way you can attempt to leave the base, it's too open, you would be seen!"

Margaret paced the floor, "Yes, I know you're right but.." a soft knock on the door.

Bram and Margaret looked at each other. Margaret asked in a whisper, "You expecting anyone?"

Bram replied, in a low voice also, "No, no one."

"Do you think we could have been heard by someone passing?"

Bram had just thought the very same thing, "I don't know. Go to the bedroom, close the door, and stay there!"

Margaret hurried to the bedroom. Bram went to the door and opened it. It was Dayton.

"Let me in, quick!" Dayton said, looking around nervously.

Bram let him in, although Dayton was already pushing past him.

"Close it, hurry!"

"What are you doing here? We're not permitted to speak with one another!"

"I know, I know, but that guy you were looking for.." Dayton was out of breathe,

"Well he's.." stopping to take in air, "I've seen him."

"What? When?"

"Today, here on the base!"

Bram regarded him with suspicion, "Why are you taking a risk coming here, to tell me this?"

"Because of what I've seen!" Dayton put his hands over his face, "Oh god, I can't get the images out of my head!"

"What the hell are you talking about?"

"I don't think I was seen coming here," he made for the window, scanning the outside of the building and surrounding area, "All clear, but they'll be starting their patrols soon, so we haven't much time."

Bram grabbed Dayton's arm, "look I don't know why you're here, but it's my turn to tell *you* to go away!"

"I'm taking a huge risk coming here!" Dayton pulled himself free of Bram's hold.

"Who asked you?"

"You did!" Dayton snapped back.

"No I didn't!"

"You asked if I'd seen your friend!"

"I never said anything about him being my friend!"

"He's my friend!"

Bram and Dayton turned to see Margaret standing in the hallway.

"I told you to stay.."

Margaret walked toward them, "I know but when I heard him say," she looked at Dayton, "that he had seen Mark today.."

Bram interrupted her, "We don't know if he can be trusted!"

"I think he can," Margaret told him, having not taken her eyes off Dayton since entering the living room. "Margaret Baker, pleased to meet you," she offered Dayton her hand.

Dayton shook her hand, "Elliot Dayton," he too had not taken his eyes off *her*.

Bram shook his head and sighed, "Now we've all been introduced, do you mind telling us why exactly you took a risk coming here!"

Dayton looked at Bram, "Yes of course."

"Sit down," Margaret indicating to the sofa.

"No, I'm fine, thank you," he gazed at her.

"Eh.hmm..Well?" Bram was irritated by Dayton's obvious starry eyed reaction to Margaret's presence.

"I saw your friend," he told Margaret. "I'm so sorry to tell you this but.," no longer able to look at her, he turned away.

"What is it?" she asked.

Bram pressed too for an answer, "Well what?"

"He's dead. I'm so sorry, but he's dead."

Bram grabbed hold of his arm and shook him, "Dead? How do you know this?"

Margaret sat down on the sofa. She had thought it best, as she felt her legs were no longer able to perform the task of keeping her upright.

"I know this because I saw it happen!" Dayton shouted to Bram, and pulled himself free of Bram's hold. He looked over at Margaret, "I really am sorry to be bringing you such terrible news."

"What happened to him?" Bram bellowed at Dayton.

"I don't think giving the full details of his death would be very tactful right now, do you?"

Bram looked over at Margaret. Returning his gaze to Dayton, he answered, "I guess not."

Margaret wept softly. Bram felt uncomfortable and was unable to find any words of comfort to offer her. Dayton seemed to know what to do though. He sat down next to her, putting his arms around her. Bram watched at the ease in which Dayton was able to console her, after having just met her.

"I know this has come as a huge shock to you. I really am sorry." Dayton asked Bram, "Is there any coffee?"

"Yes, I'll make some more now," Bram answered, pleased to be leaving the room.

He had no idea what to say to Margaret. Nothing he could say would make her feel any better right now. He still had to get her off the base, safely and very soon. But now Dayton was involved! Bram knew if she remained on the base much longer, she could jeopardise her own life, along with his and many others!

Although with Dayton on board, if he can be trusted that is, it may well be a little easier to get her out unharmed.

Bram returned with the coffee, "Here, you better drink some of this." He filled her cup and passed it to her.

"Thank you."

Bram put the coffee pot on the table, "I'll get you a cup," he told Dayton.

"No, I'm fine," replied Dayton.

Margaret asked, "Elliot, I need to know, what happened to Mark?"

Bram discerned that they were now on first name terms. "Perhaps it's best you don't ask that question right now," Bram advised her.

"He's right, you don't need to know all that right now."

"Yes I do!" she insisted.

Dayton glanced at Bram, "She's going to need to know sometime."

Bram replied, "What is important right now, is getting her off this base!"

"First, I want to know!" Margaret declared, adding, "Please Elliot just tell me."

"Okay, I'll tell you," Elliot told her.

Bram watched Margaret grip her cup tightly with both hands, her face now slightly contorted, as she held back the inevitable expressions of horror and dread, whilst learning of the precise details of her dear friend's gruesome demise.

Chapter 20

Margaret sat quietly through Elliot's horrific account of what had befallen her friend.

"He was put into a sealed capsule, wearing a suit designed to protect against high levels of the sun's radiation. Then within the sealed capsule, they reproduced other planets' atmospheric conditions," Elliot explained, "Just like the Nazi human experimentations! That's what their doing here!"

Bram was not expecting to hear anything like this, he had presumed her friend had just been shot!

Margaret wiped tears from her eyes, doing her utmost to contain her obvious distress. Bram wished he could comfort her as easily as Elliot could, but recognised his own awkwardness in such situations, "What is the purpose of these experiments?"

Elliot held Margaret's hand, "I'm so sorry," he told her, "there was no way your friend could have survived such conditions."

Bram asked, "Why not?" and added, "You said he was given a protective suit!"

Elliot looked at him, "Yes he was, but they had no intention of ending the experiment even when the suit had reached its protective limitations. They just kept increasing the levels of radiation and even introduced high levels of gases such as methane and carbon monoxide!"

Bram asked, "What the hell for?"

"Space exploration! They're going to put men into space!"

Bram was not surprised by this; he had seen the crafts, "He didn't willingly participate?"

Elliot answered, "No he did not!"

Margaret asked, "What have they done with his body? Where have they taken him?"

Bram was amazed by her composure, bearing in mind it was her friend's death Elliot was describing, "Are you okay?"

Margaret looked at Bram and replied, "Yes, yes I think so."

Elliot asked, "You sure?"

Margaret nodded that she was, "They will pay for this!" she declared.

"There's not a lot we can do.."

Margaret interrupted Bram, "What do you mean? Why not?"

"I'm afraid I have to agree with him," said Elliot.

"But they killed him! They can't get away with that!"

Both Elliot and Bram knew different. The base had its own set of laws. Within its perimeters there was only one system in place, and the rules governing that of the outside world did not apply here.

Bram shrugged his shoulders, "Not sure there's anything we can do about it right now, but perhaps.."

Margaret's grief was quickly replaced by anger and frustration, "No way are those responsible going to get away with it! They murdered him!"

"Yes they did," Elliot replied, "and they will pay for it, but right now, Bram is right, we have to get you safely out of here first!"

Margaret nodded in agreement, "Then I'm going to make sure they pay!"

"Remember if you mention us," Bram pointed to himself and Elliot, "we are still on this base!"

Elliot said, "They will want to know how you knew what happened to him."

"I don't want to get either of you in any trouble," Margaret realised that making those responsible for killing her friend, was not going to be as easy as she had first thought, "they may well get away with this." She quickly determined, "My god! They may never be brought to justice!"

Both Bram and Elliot had already ascertained this, "We just don't know how they can be made to pay for his murder, and without anyone else becoming their next victim," Elliot told her.

"It's true, whatever happens within this base, stays within the base, hell, no one can even get close to its perimeters," Bram explained.

Elliot asked her, "If you were to say anything, who would you tell?"

Margaret thought of the bigoted sheriff, "I don't know, the FBI perhaps?"

Bram answered, "They have no jurisdiction out here! Authority here comes from the very top!"

"He's right I'm afraid," said Elliot.

Margaret looked at them both in turn, the look of despondency on her face, "There must be something we can do?"

Bram was unable to lie to her, "For now, no, there is nothing we can do." He wished there was, "I'm sorry about your friend, but.."

Margaret interrupted him, "This can't be happening!"

Elliot told her, "There's nothing we can do for him now, but you need to get off this base, and before they find you here!"

Bram added, "It's dark now, you need to go now!"

"Fine I'll go, but you two promise me that when the time comes, if it ever comes that is," Margaret didn't hold much hope on it, "that you will tell the world what's been going on here!"

Elliot agreed right away, but Bram was unsure if there would ever be a time when it would be safe for them to say what was happening on the base, "When the time comes," he told her, and added, "Right, let's go!"

Elliot asked, "What have you planned?"

"Earlier I dug out a trench under the perimeter fence, not much, but deep enough for you to squeeze under, as I didn't want to stay out there too long and risk being seen."

"The fence is electrified," Elliot told Margaret.

"I know it is."

"Yes, how did you manage to get into the base?" asked Bram.

"Through that mountain!"

"What?" replied Bram and Elliot in unison.

"You heard me, and yes, I know what's going on in there too!"

Bram looked at her in disbelief, "You know?"

"Yes I know about the flying disks, and about those who flew them here!"

Elliot looked at her, amazed, "but you said nothing."

"Why would I?"

"Well it's no matter now, we have to go!" said Bram.

"I'm not going to let this go," Margaret told them, "they will pay for this, *somehow*!"

"There must be a way we can remain in contact with you on the outside," said Elliot, "I know, and it may just work too!"

Bram looked at him, "What way is that then?"

"I still have to register those I'll be corresponding to on the outside."

Margaret asked, "What do you mean, like family?"

"Yes like family members."

Bram figured what he meant, "And a girlfriend."

Elliot answered, "Exactly!"

Bram asked, "So why have you not done that already?"

"They were in a rush to get me to my assignment, said I could do it tomorrow."

"Well that's settled then, I'm your girlfriend!"

"Indeed," answered Elliot.

Bram didn't wish to witness any more of Elliot's starry eyed dazing, "Write down your address," he told Margaret, "and let's just go!"

Chapter 21

She had never been so happy to see her old beat up '53 Sedan. Margaret had hidden it well, before walking some distance to the desert base. Now off the base, and now knowing Mark was dead, Margaret was uncertain of what to do next. Mark was beyond help, and she had no idea if those responsible would ever be brought to justice.

Bram and Elliot would surely face a similar death to Mark's, if she were to write up a story for the newspaper telling how he had died on that Air base. Her life *too* would be in danger. 'Made to look like an accident,' Bram had told her. She felt angry, scared and frustrated, all at the same time. She wanted to cry, but wanted to hit out also. Margaret headed for the newspaper office.

No one was about she assumed, as the place was all locked up and she could see no lights were on. Margaret had her own key. This was not unusual, as reporters frequently came to the office after hours to write up their story, especially if they had been out interviewing all day. She sat at her desk. What could she write?

Nothing! Margaret cried.

"Where have you been?"

Margaret hadn't heard him come in, "Are you okay?" he asked.

She looked up to see her boss standing over her.

"What's wrong? Where have you been?"

Margaret tried hard to compose herself, "I've been," she wiped her eyes, "There was a family emergency, and I.,"

Her boss interrupted, "Judging by how upset you are, whatever it is, it must be serious. Want to talk about it?"

"No, it's okay, all got on top of me a little, that's all. Really I'll be fine."

"You sure? Do you need some time off?"

Margaret wanted the conversation to end, "No, I'm fine really, thank you."

"Well if you're sure."

Margaret now more composed, "Yes I am."

"That friend of yours, what's his name?"

Margaret found it hard to bring herself to say his name, afraid the tears would flow again, "His name., is Mark."

"Mark!" he affirmed.

"Yes, Mark," she fought hard to hold back the tears.

"The sheriff has listed *him* as his main suspect in the Myers' murders."

"That doesn't surprise me."

"You think he killed them?"

"No! That's not what I meant." Margaret was disgusted at the idea, "That sheriff is ignorant! He would blame a *dog* if one had been at the scene at the time of the murders!"

"Then you do admit your friend was at the scene when the murders took place?"

"Stop putting words in my mouth! You're beginning to sound like that sheriff!"

"*That sheriff,* you say, you don't like him much, do you?"

Margaret despised him, "No I don't!"

"Granted he's a little, what you might say.,"

"Bigoted!" said Margaret.

"Well I don't know if I would go as far as to say that."

"Well I would!" Margaret wanted so much to tell him her friend was dead, and show the sheriff up for the fool he was, blaming a dead man! However, she couldn't, and wouldn't put Bram and Elliot in danger, she didn't care about what happened to herself anymore. "I've got better things to worry about than that sheriff."

"You should go home and get some rest. Come in tomorrow only if you feel up to it. I hope whatever your family emergency was, that it will turn out okay."

Margaret feared it wouldn't, "Thank you. I'll be in tomorrow, I'll be fine."

"That's good, missed having you about the place," he smiled.

Margaret strained a smile in return.

"Oh, one more thing, Tom Myers, best stay out of his way!"

Margaret asked, "Why?"

"He thinks you've been helping your friend hide from the law."

"What? Mark killed no one! He doesn't need hiding from the law, he's.," She stopped, realising she was about to tell him Mark was dead.

"He's what?"

Margaret answered, "He's innocent!"

"And you're certain of that?"

"Yes I am!"

"So you've spoken to him then?"

"No, I haven't, but I know he's not responsible for killing the Myers!"

"Where is he then? Why did he just disappear after the murders? He was on their farm that day wasn't he?"

Margaret hated that anyone should think Mark to be capable of murder, "Yes he was, but he may well be dead too!"

"Do you really think so?"

Margaret just wanted the condemning of her friend to end, "Well yes I do!"

"I see, never thought of that," he replied.

"No and I'm sure the sheriff hasn't either. Too busy blaming innocent people and without any evidence too!"

"Yes well, that's our sheriff alright, guilty first," he shook his head.

"He's even blamed the people up on the old Dugan's farm!" Margaret knew, and only too well, that if she were to tell the sheriff about the Air base and how Mark had been killed, he would not have believed her anyway. He was too dim-witted to grasp what was really going on. Keeping someone like him in charge of a town close to that base, guaranteed its true activities would never be known.

"Yes I know about that, but they are a strange lot," he replied.

"Strange doesn't mean they are murderers!"

"Well, you never can tell."

Margaret realised she was wasting her time, "Whatever, I'm going to head home now," she told him. There wasn't much she could do at the office anyway.

"So I'll see you here in the morning?"

"Yes you will," Margaret answered. She said goodnight and left, unable to get Mark out of her head, or the Air base where his body now lay, and most probably having been buried out in the desert somewhere without prayer or marker. She was determined, and even at the cost of her own life, that those responsible would pay for Mark's death.

Chapter 22

Bram, having been taking back to the mountain the next morning, was informed he was to fly one of the interceptor aircrafts; the F-102.

"A test flight?" he asked.

The lieutenant replied, "No. You are to circle the desert surrounding the Air base."

"What am I looking for?"

"Any unauthorised vehicles or civilians on foot on the ground, and within a five mile radius of the Air base."

Bram asked, "Five mile? Is that necessary?"

"Yes, it's necessary. Of course that also includes any aircraft, be them civilian or foreign military."

"Soviet?"

"Whatever," replied the lieutenant.

Bram enjoyed the reaction he got from the lieutenant by asking too many questions, "What kind of unauthorised vehicles?"

"The kind that have not been given authorisation to be out here!"

"But how will I know that?"

The lieutenant was clearly irritated, "It's very simple, you report back to the tower what you see, that is all!"

Bram took great pleasure in the lieutenant's obvious exasperation, "So I don't have to know then? Just report what I see?"

"That's correct!"

"Well why didn't you just say that in the first place?" Bram answered.

The lieutenant was not impressed by Bram's obstinacy, "You know how it works!"

"What I don't understand, is why bring me *here* and not just straight to the airfield?"

The lieutenant was in no mood for any more of Bram's questions, "Get in the jeep, I'll take you there now!"

"All this back and forth stuff," Bram shook his head, "waste of time."

The lieutenant gave him a look of disapproval but said nothing. When Bram arrived at the airfield, the F-102 was nowhere to be seen.

"Where is the aircraft?"

"In the hanger," it was obvious to Bram from his tone, the lieutenant would not be entering into another quick fire round of questions with him. Besides, Bram had no intention of asking any more, having felt he'd irritated the lieutenant quite enough for one day. No further words were exchanged between them, and having left the lieutenant, Bram headed for the hanger. There, he was greeted by two ground crew.

"Whenever you're ready," one of them told Bram.

Bram was very much looking forward to getting back into the cockpit, and into the cockpit of an F-102, even better. He had not flown one of these since the Academy.

With a cruise speed of 845mph, and having to fly blind, while referencing its instruments, was no picnic, nevertheless, Bram got a real thrill from hurtling through the air at -40 degrees Fahrenheit, in air so thin that if he were to lose pressure he would have a window of only 4-5 seconds, before losing consciousness and dying. And of course the jack-o-lantern of a radar he had to carefully watch at all times, didn't help either, however, that only added to the buzz of being only seconds from death. Bram loved it!

Kitted up and rearing to go, Bram prepared the aircraft for take off. There were a few minor aerodynamic problems with the F-102's, Bram knew, like at certain power settings the jet compressor could stall sending the aircraft into an inverted roll. Bram was precise, and was not in the habit of making mistakes.

Now airborne, Bram intended to get as much adrenaline pumping through his veins as he possibly could. He flew close to the ground, watching his radar for any squiggles that would indicate something on the ground. Flying this close was suicidal, but it excited him. He soared above the desert Air base, his radar picking up nothing. Bram updated the tower, informing them that the nose-mounted infrared search and track was fully operational and that radar was picking up nothing, either in the sky above the base, or in the surrounding desert over a six mile radius. He was ordered to keep circling the area, and he didn't mind, as he was enjoying himself.

Something then showed up on radar, he wasn't sure at first, but a closer check revealed there was a small squiggle. Bram changed direction, trying to get a fix on it. He hoped, and if he could get close enough, he could perhaps get a visual. Bram flew below and at close range to it. The object was moving fast, that was a good thing, as it would be possible to get a good look without outrunning it. He was just half a mile from it now. He kept his altitude lower than the object. He had a visual and was now able to make out what it was. A flying disk, and similar to the types he had been shown on the base. Its metallic body was akin to aluminium. It was so shiny that when the sunlight caught it, it glinted brightly, blinding him so much so, it forced him to look away.

Bram followed the flying disk. He was about to inform the tower, when over his headset, he was told to cease following the disk-like craft. They were observing it from the ground, but not surprising, as it was so large, and only flying three miles up. It would not have been possible for it to have remained unseen from the ground at that altitude. Were they expecting the craft? Bram suspected they were. His timely check of the area surrounding the base was no coincidence. Now unable to follow the craft or keep it on radar, Bram had no idea where it went, or if it had landed somewhere on the base. Ten minutes after his last sighting of the craft, Bram was ordered to land the F-102.

Chapter 23

A smartly dressed man entered the meeting room, "Good to be back!" he said.

Four other men, in their tailored suits, sat round the large oak table. One of them asked him, "Anything new to report from the base?"

"Actually there's quite a lot to report on this occasion," he joined them round the table. They regarded him with interest. "Let's begin though with the problems occurring close by the base," he continued. "There seems to be some interest building with regard to patterns found in local farmers' crop fields and.."

One of the men interrupted him, "We're not interested, that can sort itself out!"

"Here here," replied some of the others.

Another spoke out, "Wait, perhaps he has a point. I read a local newspaper article, and it would seem people are taking this phenomenon very seriously indeed."

"Exactly, and as I was saying, with regard to the crop patterns and them being linked to those mutilations.."

Another then asked, "The farmer and his wife?"

"Yes. They were very well known and liked in the area, and local people are not about to let it go. Regardless of what those crop patterns mean, they believe them to be linked somehow to the murders. We need to bring a human face to these murders."

"So what you're saying is, if they have *someone* for the murders, they won't be so bothered about the crop patterns?"

"Yes, that's exactly the point I'm making. I was there, I spoke with some of the towns' people, and while the crop patterns are indeed a mystery, as long as the person or persons that committed this awful crime walks free, the crop patterns will continue to be a concern to them."

"But they are linked! How is it, that by giving them someone to blame, that it would *unlink* them?" asked another.

"They are small minded, back-water, towns' folk, they can only deal with one issue at a time. Give them a murderer and they'll get busy gathering a lynch mob!" said another of the men. The room reverberated with the sound of laughter. He had to raise his voice to be heard over them, "Look, you all elected me to go there, and that was my findings. If none of you are satisfied with that, then I can only suggest you choose another to go there, but I promise you, which ever one of you goes, the conclusion will be the same!"

Another spoke out over the laughter, "Okay, okay, let's give them what they want!" The laughter ceased. He continued, "What have you in mind?"

"The sheriff."

The men looked at each other, and one of them asked, "Don't we still need him?"

"I'm afraid there is no other way, it has to be him!"

A low mumbling in the room, as each of the men discussed the idea with the man sat next to him.

He waited for a reply, "Are we going to take a vote on it then?"

They turned their attention back to him and nodded their agreement.

"It won't be easy, however with careful planning, we should be able to give the locals more than enough evidence. The crop patterns will fade into the background and hopefully for good!

Given sufficient time they may very well turn into nothing more than local folklore."

Another asked, "And this plan, will it also end the questions of *how* and *why* the mutilations occurred?"

He replied, "Yes, it most certainly will, and with this issue laid to rest we can get on with our mission at the base."

Chapter 24

Two days had passed since she'd left the Air base. Margaret felt a growing unease amongst the towns' people, concerning the brutal murders of the kindly farmer and his wife. Margaret knew, and only too well, that the pressure on the sheriff to find the person responsible, was increasing with each passing day. Although she had no liking for him, Margaret decided to pay him a visit.

"Good morning sheriff," Margaret did not wish to get into another confrontation with him. "Any update on the Myers' murders?"

"Are you asking, or is it for the newspaper?"

Margaret sensed right away from him, that it may prove difficult to avoid another clash of opinion. "The newspaper," she lied.

"I see, well, on the record, we are doing all we can to catch whoever is responsible, and off the record, we will be questioning *your* friend!"

Just as she had suspected, "I have already told you, there is no way on god's earth Mark killed those people!"

"I wouldn't expect you to say any different."

Margaret was now regretting her decision coming to see him, "You have no evidence to suggest he did!"

"I have plenty of evidence, for one, he was the last to see them alive, and two, he hasn't been seen since. That makes him a pretty good suspect!"

The fact that he was *dead* made him a pretty poor suspect, but Margaret could only think this, "And you have no one else in mind for the murders? Are you not looking for anyone else then?"

"As a matter of fact, we are looking at others who may well have been involved."

"Others? Who?"

"Tom Myers got a whisper that your friend may well be hiding out with those hippies up on the old Duggan's farm, and although I don't agree with folk taking the law into their own hands.."

Margaret had almost forgotten the sheriff's conversation with Tom about the new owners being, in his opinion, devil worshippers. "Why would Mark be up there?

He doesn't know them, that's ridiculous!" Even more so as Mark was dead! Margaret was so frustrated at not being able to say just how impossible it was that her friend may be hiding there or *anywhere*!

"The people of this town want action, and someone to pay for this terrible crime!"

Margaret wondered who would pay for Mark's death, "So you're going to blame innocent people because they are not from this town!"

"That is not why, if your friend was innocent, why did he run away? Tom went up to the Duggan's farm, and was greeted by three men with shot guns. They forced him off their land! Now does that look like the actions of innocent people with nothing to hide?"

Margaret guessed they reacted like that because of the way the sheriff had handled the shoplifting charge of one their children, "What do you expect? The people in this town don't speak to them! Whispering to each other if they should meet one of them in the street. And you haven't exactly welcomed them either!"

"Tom Myers is a well respected man, and the son of good, hard working, law abiding citizens, that were brutally murdered in their own home! I am not about to leave any stone unturned!"

"That maybe, but you have already found Mark, and now the people living up on that farm, guilty of their murders before questioning any of them!"

"Since your *friend* has disappeared, he has made it impossible for me to question him!

As for the new owners of the Duggan's farm, I have asked them to come here for questioning, but as yet, not one of them has showed up!"

Margaret understood their reluctance to come in for questioning, but also how something like this would make an already bigoted sheriff, who was obviously on the edge, likely to do something foolish. "Why don't you go up there and speak to them?"

"I am going up there to speak to them, with my deputies. I have a warrant to search their farm for your friend."

Margaret realised that the sheriff may well intend to call a siege upon the people on that farm, "I've told you, Mark is not up there hiding out! How do you think they are going to react when they see you and all your deputies coming to their farm, especially now that Tom has been up there?"

"If they have nothing to hide, there will be no trouble, and if they had nothing to hide, why didn't they just allow Tom to search their farm in the first place?"

Margaret didn't believe for a moment that the search was going to go off peacefully.

"Why should they? It's their property! Would you like it if people turned up on your property asking to search it?"

"They knew who Tom was, and how his parents had been murdered, why not allow him to check their property?"

"It's not that simple, they're probably just angry at being suspected of something in the first place!"

"Look don't try to tell me my job, I've been dealing with criminals.."

Margaret interrupted the oncoming lecture, "when is this all supposed to happen?"

"This afternoon, and if they get wind of it before then, I'll know who told them!"

"I think you're making a big mistake sheriff, going up there with deputies and warrants!" Margaret guessed their unwillingness to allow Tom onto their land, was most probably due to the fact, they did not trust the bigoted locals *and* their dim-witted sheriff.

"I know my job, and I have nothing further to say to you."

"If they don't agree to your search of their property, what then?"

"That will be decided when, and *if* that happens."

Margaret knew she was wasting her time talking to him, and without saying anything further, she left the sheriff's office.

Chapter 25

Margaret asked her boss if she could go to the Duggan farm to speak to the new owners, and get their side of the story, but he refused.

"At the very least it could help prevent more trouble!"

Her boss asked, "How?"

"The sheriff already believes they are guilty in some way, and before he's even talked to them. This way, they can have their say before he goes up there this afternoon."

"Even if you *do* go up there and get their side, the story would not be in the paper until tomorrow morning, so how can it help with the sheriff's search of their farm today?" Margaret was hoping she could persuade them to allow the search of their property, she also intended to let them know, that she too, believed the sheriff to be nothing more than a intransigent idiot. "I just think it would help, and you would be getting a story out of it," she hoped by saying this, it might help sway him. He didn't answer, perhaps she had a chance of persuading him after all, "It can't hurt. If they are guilty of the murders, which I doubt, then you would have gotten an interview with them long before any trial began!" Margaret was desperate now, "Please, why would you let this opportunity go? If the sheriff does arrest any of them, then it'll be highly unlikely we'd ever get an interview with any of them!"

"Okay go, interview them, but until the sheriff has ruled them out of the murders, whatever they say will not be printed!"

Margaret didn't care if the interview never got into the newspaper, her motive for the interview was to try and calm the situation, and before it had the opportunity to get out of hand. They needed to know that they were not alone in thinking the sheriff was an inherent fool.

"Understood!" Margaret couldn't wait to get to the farm, "I'll go right away!"

"Before you go, a letter arrived for you, your landlady dropped it by, thought it might be urgent, as the markings on the envelope showed it had come from that Air base not far from here."

Bram., Elliot., they had kept their promise to remain in touch, "Where is it?"

"I left it on your desk. Is it something important?" He looked at her curiously, "Why would you be receiving correspondence from that Air base? You working on something?"

"No. No, of course not, it's a guy I'm seeing, he's posted there," that's what Elliot had told his commanders on the Air base, and she was not going to say any different.

"You never said you were seeing anyone."

"Why would I?"

"Mmm., I suppose. Judging by your reaction to the arrival of that letter, you must be quite fond of him. Seeing him long?"

Margaret was surprised by his interest in her love life, "No not long." She felt uncomfortable about lying, "Better get a move on if I'm to get to the farm before the sheriff."

"Indeed, so go to it then."

"Right away!" Margaret headed straight to her desk, she didn't wish to wait until after the interview to read the letter. She picked it up and opened it.

Dear Margaret, we are fine, and happy to know you are no longer in any danger. Margaret knew that *we,* meant Elliott and Bram, and that by, *any danger*, he meant that she was no longer on the Air base.

Nothing different to report home about, other than what you already know. Just need to know you are alright. I am sorry about your friend. Will do all that is possible to help make it right. I promise you that.

Margaret understood the difficult predicament he and Bram were in, and she didn't want any harm to come to them. Mark had been her closet and dearest friend, nevertheless, she acknowledged the risk to Bram's and Elliot's lives, as well as her own, if she were to inform the authorities that she knew he was dead. The first question asked would be, *how are you so sure he's dead?* What could she answer?

I am not going to make this a long letter, as you know I've only been on the base a short while, I guess a week can seem a lot longer, when away from loved ones.

'A week,' they've only been there a week! Margaret hadn't thought to ask them that.

I hope you are able to remain strong through your loss, and I want you to know that, although it is impossible for me to make it better for you now, I will never forget, and one day your wish will be granted. Don't lose hope.

Margaret knew he meant it. She wondered if it was safe to send letters. Both Elliot and Bram had said that it was, as to send any information regarding their activities on the base, would ensure to put their's and their loved one's lives in jeopardy.

Nevertheless, she had an uneasy feeling about it.

"You maybe a little too late!"

Startled, Margaret looked up to see her boss standing next to her desk, she hadn't heard him come into the room, "What do you mean?"

"Think the sheriff may have given you the wrong information."

Margaret had no idea what he was talking about, "What wrong information? Too late for what?"

"This afternoon, you said."

Margaret suddenly realised what he was telling her, "He lied! He's gone up there now isn't he?"

"Yes, and with all his deputies too," he answered.

Margaret got to her feet, "That son-of-a-bitch!"

"Wow, didn't know you used language like that!"

She picked up the letter, folded it, and put it into her pocket, "Only when I'm *really* pissed!"

"Guess he's not your favourite person today."

Margaret was furious, "He never was!"

"Where are you going?"

"To the farm!"

"I don't think that's a good idea."

"And why not?"

"Because I don't think this is going to go down very well. Ever since one of those hippie kids got a five-fingered-discount from the general store in town, he's had it in for them!"

Margaret stood at the door, "So what you're saying is, that because a kid was caught stealing some candy, his family are all murderers?"

"No of course I'm not saying that, but you know our sheriff, anyone remotely different and he's.."

Margaret finished his sentence, "He's an idiot!"

"That's not what I was about to say! He's just a little tightly wound is all."

"A badass, dumb cop with a vendetta, and who's looking for someone to blame, is what you'd call, a little tightly wound?"

"Folk round here want to know who killed two of their neighbours, and they were good people too, the Myers never harmed anyone. Your friend has gone missing.."

"He had nothing to do with those murders!"

"I never said he did, but maybe he's dead too! And the only thing that's changed around here prior to those murders, is that they moved here. Those crop patterns, and the Myers, brutally murdered in their home, all occurred *after* they came here!"

Margaret knew there was no point continuing to argue with him, and besides, she had to get to that farm, and quick! "I'm going to the farm!"

"I can't talk you out of it?"

"No you can't!"

"Be careful! I'll be expecting a good story for the morning paper!"

Margaret wasn't concerned about getting a story, she was more worried about the sheriff declaring a siege on the farm and its owners.

Chapter 26

By the time Margaret reached the farm, there was already a stand off between the owners and the sheriff.

She asked one of the deputies what was happening, but he didn't respond, only regarding her with disapproval. She asked again, and louder this time, "What's going on?"

He didn't answer her question, "You here for a story?"

"No! I mean, yes., look, what's happening? Why has the sheriff surrounded the farm?"

"Have a warrant to search the property, those hippies are not allowing us on their farm," his loaded shotgun pointed toward the farmhouse.

"Where is the sheriff?"

The deputy glared toward the farmhouse, "He's up there."

"What? In the farmhouse?"

"No. He's laying low, behind that tree close to the porch."

Margaret could see the tree, but not the sheriff, "I don't see him, and besides, why is he hiding? Why not just go knock on the front door?"

The deputy turned his gaze to her, "That's what he was about to do, until one of those hippies came out onto the porch pointing a gun at him, and shouting to us to get off his property!"

Margaret suspected the sheriff had approached the farmhouse with his gun on show, making it obvious how he felt about them, "Let me go up there. I'll talk to them."

He mocked, "You? Why? Are you a reporter or a negotiator?"

She ignored his sarcasm, "Look, the sheriff's only making things worse, and anyway it's my friend he thinks they're hiding up there!"

"Sheriff's up there," the deputy returned his gaze to the farmhouse, "can't ask him now anyways." She had already decided she was going, and walked away from the deputy, "I'm going up there! And no one is going to stop me!"

The deputy shouted to her, "Hey! You can't go up there!"

"Watch me!"

As she got closer to the house, Margret could see the sheriff lying in the deep grass behind the tree. The tree, she guessed, was roughly about ten or twelve yards from the porch. At the bottom of the porch steps Margaret looked again toward the tree.

She called out to him, "Sheriff!" Although she knew for sure Mark was not in the farmhouse, she said, "I'm going to ask to speak with them. If Mark *is* here, then he won't hide from me."

The sheriff replied, "You should not be here! Don't interfere with the law!"

"I am not trying to interfere sheriff, but I do think you are only making matters worse!"

The door of the farmhouse opened slightly, "Who are you? What do you want?"

Margaret ascended the steps of the porch, "My name is Margaret Baker, I work for the local newspaper, and like you I'm not from these parts," she hoped by saying that she was not one of the local citizens, they might be less wary of her.

He asked, "What is it you want?"

"It's my friend the sheriff is looking for."

"Like I've told him, he's not here!"

Margaret was only a few feet from the door, "I know he's not. That's why I'm here. Please let me talk with you for a moment." Softly now, so as not to permit the sheriff to hear, "I too know the sheriff is nothing more than a fool. Please let me talk to you inside."

The door opened a little more, the man regarded her with suspicion, "Okay we'll talk to you, but not that sheriff!"

Margaret called back to the sheriff, "Just give me a moment sheriff before you do anything, I'm going to speak with them!"

He replied, "I told you not to get in the way!"

Ignoring him, Margaret entered the farmhouse. There were six adults, three women and three men. The men all wore shabby clothes and sported beards. The women wore maxi dresses and all had long hair. Margaret knew they were not the murdering kind, as the hippie culture represented peace, love and freedom. Although she was also well aware of how much they were against established structures, such as the church, governments and the *law*.

The children were nowhere to be seen, "Hi I'm Margaret," she told them. "I'm from Fresno, and I'm a journalist for the local newspaper."

Only the man who let her in spoke, "Why does he think your friend is here?"

"You've all heard about the Myers' murders?"

One of the women spoke up, "Yes, but what has that got to do with us?"

Margaret turned to look at her, "Nothing, absolutely nothing! But as you're new in town and.."

The woman interrupted, "We're devil worshippers, right?"

"That's not what *everyone* believes," Margaret assured her.

The woman replied, "But your sheriff believes that's what we are!"

"Like I said, he's ignorant," Margaret told her.

"Sit down," said another of the women.

"Thank you."

The same woman asked, "Why have you come here, if you don't think your friend is here? And what is he wanted for?"

"It's because I know he's not here that I've come, and I also know what that sheriff is capable of. The sheriff has made him his prime suspect in the murders."

She replied, "Us too, by the looks of it!"

Margaret asked, "Why not just allow him to carry out his search? You have nothing to hide, Mark's not here."

The man who had let Margaret in, answered, "This is our pad, and we've already told him your friend's not here!"

"I know, but he has a warrant, and that gives him the right to search your farm. He won't go away until he has searched your property!"

"Maybe she's right, we should just allow the search, and then he'll leave us alone," said another of the women.

He replied, "Then every time something happens round here, they'll come bothering us! We have to show them that we won't be pushed around."

Margaret asked, "Don't you have children?" They all looked at one another. "You don't want trouble from the law with young children about."

"She's right," said the same woman. "He's not going to go away until he's carried out his search, and the children, we.." she began to cry. The two other women comforted her. The three men spoke quietly to each other, before one of them said, "Fine, you tell the sheriff there's no need for the guns, he can do his search!"

Margaret was relieved to hear this, "Great, I'll tell him. I do understand how you feel about him. My opinion of the sheriff is much the same as yours." Margaret stood up and walked toward the door, "Where are the children?" she asked.

"Upstairs," answered one of the men.

"I see, probably best to keep them next to you during the search," she told them.

Margaret left the farmhouse. She told the sheriff the owners had agreed he could carry out the search of their farm. It was not well received.

Chapter 27

Margaret decided to stay on at the farm until the search had been carried out, as she distrusted the sheriff. With the owners of the farm, and their children, now gathered in the kitchen of their farmhouse, the sheriff ordered his deputies to begin the search. Margaret waited on the porch, where she had been told to, by the sheriff.

"I don't want you getting in the way!"

"Like I said, I'm only here to help."

"Your help is no longer required. In fact, it was never required in the first place!"

She knew she had only wound him up further by speaking with the farm owners, "I was only trying to help, sheriff."

He could not hide his rage, "No, you were trying to interfere!"

Margaret trusted he would calm down once the search had been completed, she hoped so, "I'm sorry you feel that way, sheriff, but my intentions were never to interfere."

Nonetheless, she didn't intend to irritate him further.

"You just stay out of my way!"

She realised it was wise to say no more to him. He stormed past her, and entered the farmhouse. Margaret could hear him shouting instructions to his deputies on where best to begin their search. He sent all but one of them to search the outer farm buildings.

"Three families living in the same house, just aint right!" said one of the deputies, as he passed Margaret on the porch. Their small-mindedness sickened her. She then heard the sheriff order the families to go and wait outside. Margaret could now hear raised voices from some of the members of the three families, "This is our house!

Your warrant says nothing about us having to stay out of our home!" Some of the children could now be heard crying, as the sheriff bellowed at them not to argue with him. Margaret thought it best to go in, and try calm the situation, but when she got to the door, one of the deputies appeared. "It's best you wait out here Miss," he told her.

"The sheriff's only making things worse!"

"He's only doing his job Miss." He blocked the doorway with his body.

"He's making it worse I tell you!"

"Calm down Miss."

His condescending tone infuriated her, "I'm not the one who needs to calm down deputy, it's your idiotic and intolerant sheriff that needs to calm down!"

"No need for insults Miss. You will be arrested if you don't go away from this door quietly." He held her back, calling to another deputy to have her removed from the farm. Margaret could hear more raised voices coming from inside the farmhouse.

The sound of the children crying had also grown louder. "Just go in there and calm him down!" she shouted to the deputy in the doorway, as another pulled her away, and down the porch steps. "I'm not leaving!" Margaret was well aware of the fact, that not *only* did the sheriff and his deputies have guns, but so had the farm owners!

"Yes you are Miss," the deputy told her.

"What are you going to do, arrest me? For what?"

"We'll worry about that later Miss," he replied.

"You can't do that! Tell me now why I'm being arrested!"

The deputy didn't answer her, just handcuffed her and led her away.

"Look I don't care what you do to me, but those people, they've done nothing!"

Margaret wanted desperately to help them. The sheriff was volatile, like an unstable bomb, and about to explode. "Please, someone needs to stop him!"

"You stay here, Miss," the deputy put her into the back seat of the patrol car and locked the doors.

"You can't do this! I've done nothing!" she knew it was hopeless. She watched as the deputy returned to the farmhouse. Locked inside the patrol car, and with her hands in cuffs, Margaret could do nothing. Why hadn't she thought of asking the family to wait outside the farmhouse, and well away from the sheriff? If anything happens to them, and to those poor children, she would never forgive herself. She could do nothing but stare up at the farmhouse, and hope no harm would come to them.

A moment later, Margaret observed the deputies the sheriff had sent to search the outhouses and barn, now running toward the farmhouse. What was happening? She was unable to see clearly, the front of the farmhouse. "Let me out!" she cried out frantically, to no avail. "That lunatic is going to kill someone!" But no one was around to hear her. She truly believed that had her situation been different at that moment, and she was not handcuffed and locked inside the patrol car, she could have easily found it within herself to kill that crazy son-of-a-bitch! Margaret could only watch, as the deputies disappeared into the farmhouse. She wanted desperately to know that the owners and their children were okay.

She stared up at the farmhouse, praying that no one would be hurt, or worse, *killed*. Although if anyone was to be injured or *killed*, she hoped it would be the sheriff! Just then she saw two of the deputies emerge from the farmhouse with one of the farm owners. He was flanked by the two deputies, his head bowed, with the sheriff walking behind him, his gun pointing to his back. Margaret watched as they came closer to the patrol car.

The man kept his face down, and like her, he was handcuffed. The deputies put him into another of the patrol cars. "Let me out!" Margaret yelled to them. The sheriff approached her, and unlocked the door, "I'm going to let you go, but I should put you in the cells for the night!"

"For what? I didn't do anything!"

He helped her out of the car, and turned her around to open the handcuffs, "I told you not to get in my way!"

With the cuffs now off, Margaret rubbed at her sore wrists, "You sheriff, are a maniac! You are going to kill someone!"

The sheriff laughed, "Only the bad guys, Miss."

"They have done nothing! Why are you arresting him?" Margaret pointed to the man in the patrol car, she recognised him as the one who had shown her into the farmhouse earlier, "What has he done?"

"He *too* was interfering with me carrying out my job!" The sheriff now no longer laughing, "These hippies think they don't have to abide by the law, but they'll learn that they have to, just like everyone else!"

Margaret reviled him so, "I think sheriff, you are either on some power trip, or just plain crazy!" she knew she was dicing with the devil speaking to him in that way, nevertheless, she just wasn't capable of stopping herself.

"Would you like to join him? I've got plenty of room in the cells."

Margaret thought it best to relinquish from any further admonishment.

"As I thought. Good day to you Miss," the sheriff said, and walked away.

Margaret asked one of the deputies, "What happened?"

He looked toward the sheriff nervously, and then turning to her, "The sheriff wanted them to leave the farmhouse but they refused." He glanced over at the sheriff again before continuing, "He then ordered them out at gun point, and that one," the deputy gestured to the man they had arrested, "grabbed the sheriff's gun. Said he didn't like him pointing a gun at his family."

Margaret replied, "That's understandable."

"The sheriff didn't think so."

"No, he wouldn't! What's going to happen to him now?"

The deputy looked uncomfortable, "Look it's best you stay out of this."

"Why should I? It's in the interest of this town to know what kind of man their sheriff is!"

"They already know!"

Margaret was surprised at the deputy's answer, "So why don't they do something about it, and get rid of him?"

"He's a good man, he gives the people of this town what they want. I have nothing further to say to you!"

"He gives them what they want? What the hell is that supposed to mean?"

The deputy didn't answer. He walked away. But Margaret wanted to know what he had meant, "I asked you.."

He turned to her, and in a low, but stern voice, he told her, "Leave it! I have nothing more to say to you!"

Margaret thought it best to leave it, albeit for now.

Chapter 28

Margaret returned to the newspaper office. She was still fuming at how she'd been treated. The sheriff was losing it for sure. He could easily have lost it and killed someone in that family! Elliot's and Bram's safety were *now* not her only concern. Elliot's letter, she remembered she had put it into her pocket before going to the farm.

Unfolding it, she began to read it from the beginning, although she was finding it difficult to focus on its contents after what had happened that morning. What had the deputy meant when he had said, the sheriff gives the town's people what they want? What ever did he mean? Maybe he meant the sheriff regarded strangers in the same way as they did? Although, she wondered if there was more to it than simple narrow-mindedness! All the same, she had seen the same attitude in the town's people on a number of occasions, and although they did not exhibit any signs of being crazy, or even delusional, as like their sheriff, they *too* were just as bigoted as he was. And she had never known a more loathsome person than him!

Her boss entered her office, "How did the search of the hippies' farm go?"

She was in no mood for any more expressions of intolerance, "The *hippies* as you call them, are people too, and as such, deserve to be treated like any other decent human beings should be treated!"

"It didn't go well then?" He ignored her statement, "Those sort of people don't think they have to abide by the same laws as every one else."

Margaret would not be drawn into another, to-and-fro argument, with one more narrow-minded individual. "It went as well as I'd expect, considering who was in charge."

"Well he's only doing his job, and you ought to remember that. Have you got a story for tomorrow's paper?"

Margaret knew exactly the sort of story she would like to write, however, it would not be one her boss would be much pleased with. "Only a piece about the sheriff finding nothing at the *hippies*' farm. Oh, and of course, that they were not hiding Mark on their farm after all!"

"The mystery continues," her boss replied. "One thing, didn't one of those hippies get arrested? You going to mention that too?"

Margaret knew he was being sarcastic, "Yes, I'm going to mention it *and* the reason why!"

"Just don't put yourself in the firing line is all."

"What do you mean?"

"This is a small town, folk round here know each other, trust each other, and when someone new arrives, well it takes a while for them to gain that same trust. You ought not to side with those that exhibit obvious disrespect for the law."

Margaret *too* had no respect for the town's law enforcer, "I'm not taking sides, just telling it how it is!"

"Some may not see it that way, and I don't want to see my newspaper brought into any disagreements you may have with our sheriff!"

Her hands were tied, everywhere she turned, her hands were tied. First Mark, and those who had killed him, and now the sheriff! "My story will not include any of my personal feelings for him, I can assure you."

"Glad to hear it. I'll let you get on with it," he left her office.

Margaret sat a while. She didn't want to think anymore. Her mind now her enemy.

She needed to *do* something not *think!* She was a journalist, she was going to *be* a journalist! Find out all she could about the Air base, who was in charge; names, she needed names! There was so much she needed to investigate, and she had seen a lot more on that base than she had confessed to Bram and Elliott. She decided to do as much research as possible, and then, she would return to the Air base.

Chapter 29

It was well after seven in the evening when Bram returned to his quarters. He had sat contemplating all he had observed on the base since his arrival. There certainly was a lot to take in; aliens, alien craft, human experimentation, and who exactly was in command of the Air base? The Air base commanders, the Colonel, and whoever else was responsible for making sure its top secret status remained unchallenged. The Colonel had remembered his father, although Bram was not surprised by that, as his father had mentioned the Colonel many times. Even after all these years, Bram still missed his father dearly. Bram heard a faint knock on the door. He went to the window and saw that it was Elliot. Bram went to the door and opened it.

"Are you going to let me in?" asked a nervous looking Elliot.

Bram moved out of the way to allow him in, "You are going to get us both killed!"

"I was careful. Anyway the patrols don't start for another few hours and we have to talk," said Elliott

"What about?"

"Are you kidding me? What about?"

Bram knew only too well what he wanted, "We've already been over all that, and there is nothing we can do!" He felt it would do no good to keep bringing it up.

"Yes, I know we have, but unless we keep each other informed of our assignments.."

Bram interrupted him, "What will that do? How will that help?"

"I don't know, but we promised her!"

"No, *you* promised her!"

"What are you saying, that you're not going to do anything?"

"I never said that either, but right now there's nothing we can do, and you coming here will only make things worse!"

Elliot asked, "How?"

"What do you think would happen if you were seen coming here? You heard the Colonel, no discussing our assignments with one another!"

"I won't be seen, I'll make sure of that!"

Bram asked him, "What's in this for you anyway?" Although he already knew the answer. Bram had seen the look in Elliot's face when he'd first set eyes on her.

"I'm not in it for anything other than doing the right thing! I saw her friend being killed! No one should get away with that, especially not our own government!"

"So you think it's the government that's in charge of operations here?"

"Don't you?"

Bram replied, "I'm not totally sure that is the case."

"It's the Air force, so it's the government, the Air force *belongs* to the government!"

"That maybe so, but the operations being carried out here, are not like that on any other Air base."

"No, they are not. So what are you thinking?"

"Not sure of that either, but maybe only a handful of government officials are aware of what *precisely* is going on here, all others having being informed that it's just another Air base. It stands to reason that not everyone would be briefed on it, as how else could they maintain such top level secrecy?"

"You've got a point," said Elliot. "Still, government officials come and go, and how do they prevent those no longer members of government, from telling anyone?"

Bram answered, "Threaten their lives, or the lives of their loved ones."

"That's a lot of people to threaten! I just don't buy it!"

Bram also didn't think it would be possible to threaten so many people, and over so many years, someone was bound to let it out, "Who ever is really in charge of things around here, and how ever they are managing to keep it all under wraps for all this time, I don't know, but I do know and for sure, that they are not to be messed with!"

Elliot agreed with Bram and added, "I suggest we inform each other of what we're working on, and maybe by finding out exactly the true purpose of this base, we can discover who exactly is calling all the shots!"

"And Margaret? How do you suppose we help her?"

Elliot answered, "I don't know, but at the very least, if we do find out who is in charge here, then she would have a name to go on!"

"And what will she do with that name? Who will she tell? And if she does tell someone, won't she too be killed?"

Elliot's frustration was obvious, "I just don't know!"

Bram knew, and from the beginning, that there was nothing either of them could do.

"Her friend is dead, I know how that kind of loss feels, but as I said before, there is nothing anyone can do!"

"I think she knows it too," said Elliot.

"I *too* would like to know who *exactly* is in charge around here. I think the Colonel knows a lot more about that than anyone else on this base."

"You won't get anything out of him!"

"I wouldn't expect to," answered Bram.

"I sent her a letter," Elliot told him.

"What for?"

"I don't want her to think she is on her own, and besides, we agreed we would keep in touch."

"I just don't think it's a good idea. I mean, if they were to find out you were corresponding with a local reporter.."

Elliot said, "They won't!"

"Well, let's hope not!"

"We'll keep each other updated, agreed?"

Bram felt Elliot was being unrealistic about being able to do *anything* to help Margaret, but he understood why Elliot wanted to help her. Nevertheless, it couldn't harm Bram to have at least one ally on the Air base. "Yes, agreed."

Chapter 30

A day later, Elliot met with Bram to discuss his new assignment. "It just gets worse!"

"The gravity tests? I've heard some of the scientists speaking about them," said Bram.

Elliot replied, "Bet they never mentioned they were carrying out these gravity tests on human test subjects!"

"Really? Where are they getting all these people from to carry out their tests?"

Bram guessed that wherever they came from, they were not willing participants.

"And what are these tests for exactly, do you know?"

Elliot answered, "All I've been told is that these people are terminally ill, and in return for financially taking care of their loved ones after they have gone, they are willing to partake in these experiments."

"Do you believe that?"

"Well, whatever I believe, the important thing is *they* believe it!"

Bram replied, "That's true. What happens during these tests?"

"I couldn't mention in any detail before, because Margaret was here, as it was one of these experiments that resulted in the death of her friend," said Elliott.

"She's not here now, so what happened?"

Elliot took a moment before answering. "The scientists were, and from what I could gather, trying to discover what effect conditions on other planets in our solar system, would have, on the human body."

"Yes, I recall you mentioning specially designed suits for this," said Bram.

"That's right, space suits. One such experiment, and the one to which was carried out on Mark, was testing the effects of too much gravity on the human body. The suit did nothing to protect him, all the blood in his upper body was forced down and right out of him! It was horrific!"

Bram knew Mark would have died violently, but could never have guessed just how cruelly he had met his end, "So glad you didn't reveal that to Margaret."

"I couldn't tell her, that image will never leave me!"

"The scientists, they are attempting to design a suit that overcomes the effects caused by different measures of gravity? Why?"

Elliot answered, "For space travel! They intend to put men in space."

"Yes, I am aware of the race to the moon, but to *planets*, that's not one I've ever heard mentioned before."

"Not meant to!" Elliot replied. "It's like in those concentration camps, the Nazi experiments, and have you noticed how some of the scientists here are German?"

Bram realised that he hadn't, until now, "No, but come to mention it, nearly all of them are."

Elliot asked, "That's right! What do you make of it?"

"These experiments, have you heard anything else other than the gravity thing?"

"Genetically engineered human type!"

Bram looked at Elliot puzzled, "What does that mean?"

"That's what I've heard the scientists speak of," Elliot told him.

"But what does that mean?"

"A species of human that could live on another planet! A species of their own creation!"

"And that's happening here?"

"Yes. They spoke of gene manipulation, and finding certain genes in the human body. They select those required to create a human type that could survive on another planet."

Bram looked at Elliot in disbelief, "Playing God?"

"If you like, yes, playing God," Eliot replied. "Apparently, during the war in Europe there was talk of the Germans building flying saucers, do you recall hearing about that?"

"Yes I do," Bram answered.

"You and Margaret both saw the flying disks in that mountain."

"Some of those flying disks I saw did look too ridiculous to have been built by any alien."

"Well, I think they may have been recovered after the war and brought here, along with some of the Nazi scientists. There are other intelligent life forms other than us humans, that's for certain, and although I've not seen any of these crafts, I don't believe that they all came from aliens!"

Bram asked, "What does all this add up to, do you think?"

"I'm not really sure."

Bram thought for a moment. "Alien crafts, experiments on human test subjects, perhaps the government, or whoever is really in command of this Air base, is attempting to not only put man in space, but to colonise another planet. To put a base there, and with the help of our alien visitors." Bram knew how impossible that would have seemed to him before his arrival on the base, but not now.

"Even if that were true, whatever for?"

"I have no idea, and besides, I've not come here for that," Bram answered.

"What do you mean, you've not come here for that?"

Bram realised how that must have sounded to Elliot, "I mean, I came here to fly aircraft and nothing more!"

"I came here as an engineer, and I end up being involved in engineering people!"

"Changing the subject altogether, have you heard anything from Margaret?"

Elliot replied that he hadn't.

"All this information we're gathering, do you intend to tell her, and what do you think she will do with it?"

"I don't know, I hadn't thought that far ahead," Elliot answered.

"I see, you do know it won't help bring back her friend."

"Yes I do, and I think she does too, but that's all part of the healing."

"What is?"

"Doing something, or at least feeling like you are."

"Well if she thinks she can inform the authorities about what is going on here.."

Elliot interrupted, "She wouldn't do that, she wouldn't put us in any danger, you heard her!"

"Yes, I did, but desperation can make us do irrational things."

"Nothing about her makes me believe her to be irrational."

Bram had figured he would defend her, "Indeed, but we are dead men for sure, if she should say anything, and to anyone!"

"I do know that, and I'm positive she does too!"

Bram still wasn't convinced, "Chain of command."

"What?" asked Elliot.

"I would like to discover the chain of command around here."

"Colonel Maxwell," Elliot replied. "He gives the orders."

"Yes, well we can't be too sure of that, I mean he could only be carrying out the orders of someone higher up, someone we've not yet met."

"Of course he is! That's how it works isn't it? The chain of command. You said it yourself," answered Elliot.

"Are we going around in circles here? The Colonel may well be carrying out orders from his superiors, but there are certain decisions he must have made by himself!"

"What does that matter?"

Elliot was beginning to irritate him, "Look, it matters okay, there must have been decisions made that only *he* was responsible for!"

"Why does that matter?"

"Forget it," Bram no longer wanted to continue with the issue. "You better go, the patrols will begin shortly."

Elliot left Bram with his thoughts.

Chapter 31

Feeling emotionally charged from the days events, Margaret remained at the office long after everyone had gone home for the evening, preferring the office environment to write up her story for the morning paper. Having struggled with it for many hours, she finally got everything essential down on paper, being careful of course, not to offend anyone, the sheriff in particular. Not that she concerned herself with hurting the sheriff's feelings, but her boss was right, he had a lot of supporters in the town, and she didn't wish to clash with anyone else!

Leaving her story on the chief editor's desk, where it would be collected for printing, Margaret left the office. After locking up, she decided to drop by the sheriff's office to see how his prisoner was getting along. While she didn't much fancy having to see the sheriff again that day, or what's more, any other day, nevertheless, she needed to know that the innocent man he held in one of his cells, was all right. She figured the sheriff would not hold him there any longer than one night, just long enough to teach him a lesson.

It was late, so Margaret was not surprised to see no deputies about when she entered the sheriff's office. The sheriff was not at his desk, but she was sure he would be about somewhere. "Sheriff!" Margaret called out, "Are you here sheriff?" She peered round the door and into the corridor that led to the cells, "Sheriff, you down there?" No answer. She walked along the corridor, checking each of the rooms that led off on both sides. No one, she couldn't find anyone. "Sheriff!"

She continued down the corridor until she came to the cells. "Sheriff are you in there?" There were four cells along the left side of a narrow corridor, all six by eight, and unremarkable. Passing the first two cells, Margaret noted that there was not a sound from the sheriff's prisoner. There were only two cells left to check, but surely if the man was in one of them, he would have answered her. "Anyone? Is there anyone here?" Only one cell remained, and expecting to see the detained man inside, "Hello!" she called out as she looked into the cell, the door of which was wide open. There was someone in there, but not who she had expected to see in there; it was the sheriff! The full horror instantly seized hold of her, "Oh god no!" Even in the low lighting, she could still discern that the sheriff was dead! He couldn't possibly be alive. His lifeless body was laid out on the bed, his body having been mutilated, identical to the Myers'. His lower jaw, now torn off, lay hanging to one side, his eyeless sockets open in terror, and his belly cut open revealing a dark void within; his organs having been removed. A nauseous wave overwhelmed her. She became quite dizzy from it, and tried to steady herself by leaning against the bars of the open cell door.

There was no blood anywhere! Everything about the scene was just as it had been, when she had discovered Frank and his wife. "The sheriff's prisoner!" she said aloud, "Where was he?" Margaret needed to get away from there; from the awful grizzly spectacle. She ran from the building, hoping she had not been seen. IIt would look very suspicious if, after the sheriff's body had been discovered, someone were to say they had seen her running away from his office. But she wanted to put as much distance as possible between herself and the mutilated sheriff. Where was she going? she asked herself. To the old Duggan farm, she asserted, to check if he was there, and more importantly, to see if he had seen anything. There was no way he had anything to do with the sheriff's murder, of that she was sure, although the people of the town were unlikely to believe that!

Driving up to the farmhouse, Margaret could just make out a faint light from within. Someone was up, that was good, as no matter how urgently she wished to speak to them, she was not keen on having to wake up the household. She parked her car around the back of the house. She had no idea why, but it had seemed to her at that moment, the best thing to do. She then hurried round to the front porch and up the steps to the door. The door opened, "What do you want at this time of night?"

They had heard her drive up to the farmhouse, "You, you're okay!" It was the man the sheriff had arrested.

He regarded her curiously, "Yes, I'm fine. Why wouldn't I be?"

"The sheriff, he's dead!"

"What?"

A woman appeared in the doorway, "Margaret, isn't it?"

"Yes, that's right."

"What is she doing here?"

The man replied, "The sheriff's dead."

Margaret looked at her, "That's right. He's been murdered!"

The woman asked, "What's that got to do with us?"

"Yes, why are you telling us this?" asked the man.

"Please can I come in?"

"Let her in," said the woman. He pushed open the door to allow her inside. The rest of the women and men were sat in the living room. None of them spoke to her. "Hello again," Margaret said.

"Max had nothing to do with any murder!" said the woman who had let her in.

"Who?" asked Margaret.

"My husband," the woman pointed to the man the sheriff had earlier arrested.

"Oh, I see. I didn't know your name," Margaret answered.

"My name's Willow, I'm Max's wife."

The woman then went on to give Margaret the names of all the others. "This is Pippa and her husband Ash, and Jodi, and his wife Beth."

Margaret again said hello. They nodded but said nothing.

Willow again asked why Margaret had come to their farm, and at that time of night.

"I found the sheriff, he's dead. Killed in the same way as the Myers," she told them.

Willow replied, "Like I said, what has that got to do with us?"

"We're pretty tired of been.."

Margaret interrupted her, "No, I'm not here because I think any of you had anything to do with the murders!"

Beth asked, "Why then have you come here? And why did you park your car out back?"

"I don't know why I did, I just did is all. I came here because I needed to know Max was all right, not to accuse him of anything." Margaret turned to Max, "Did you see anything or anyone? Who let you out?"

"That's a lot of questions from someone who doesn't think I'm guilty of anything!"

"I don't think you're guilty of anything, but I need to know if you saw anything!"

"Look, when I left, and the sheriff let me go, he was alive and his usual ill-bred self!"

"And you saw no one else?"

"No, no one. The deputies had all gone home, it was just me and the sheriff."

Margaret was afraid he might say that, "You know they will come here looking to speak to you?"

Willow asked, "Who will? And what for?" She stood close to her husband, putting her arm around his waist. He held her close to him.

"The law will come. Your husband was the last to see the sheriff alive!"

Chapter 32

"What is so urgent that you need to get me up at this hour?"

The deputy replied, "Sorry Mayor, but it's the sheriff.,"

"Calm down, and just tell me what has happened deputy!"

The deputy swallowed hard, "he's dead!" He struggled to catch his breathe.

"Dead? Who?"

"The sheriff! I found him., in one of the cells.,"

The Mayor regarded him curiously, "What the hell was he doing in there?"

"I don't know, but he'd been murdered!"

"Murdered?"

"Yes, and in the same way as Harriet and Frank!"

"I'll come with you now, but let me get dressed first. Go sit down in the parlour, you can wait for me in there."

The deputy did as the Mayor instructed, unable to sit or calm himself, he instead, paced the floor. *The sheriff,* they had killed him! They would not get away with it, evidence or no evidence. The Mayor appeared in the doorway.

"Let's go deputy!"

He led the Mayor to the waiting patrol car. "It was them Sir!"

The Mayor enquired to whom he meant, "Them?"

"The hippies that bought the old Duggan's farm!"

"Oh yes, the people the sheriff spoke to me about last week."

"Then he told you?"

"If you mean, did he tell me that he suspected they were involved with the Myers' murders, then yes, he did."

"He was right! One of them was locked up in that very cell, and now he's gone, and the sheriff is dead!"

The Mayor looked at him, "He also told me that he believed them to be part of some cult. Do you know anything about that deputy?"

"Yes Sir, I do! You only have too look at how they killed the Myers, and now the sheriff, to know that! I mean why else would they remove body parts?"

"Folk round here don't like them much, do they deputy?"

"No Sir, they don't! But not without good reason Sir."

"One of their children stole from the general store, I believe."

"Yes that's right, and when the sheriff went to their farm about the incident, they warned him to stay off their land!"

"No respect for the law," said the Mayor.

"No Sir, none at all!"

"The sheriff also believed they were hiding out that new reporter's friend, is that right deputy?"

"Yes that's right. Tom Myer went up there to speak to them, but they forced him off their farm at gunpoint!"

"Mmm., not really the actions of innocent people. Tonight we'll pay them a visit. Have you rounded up the rest of the deputies?"

"Yes Sir, I have. They're at the station now."

The Mayor answered, "Good. The sooner we get to that farm the better. We can't waste any time!"

"That's what I was thinking Sir."

"By the way they reacted before, I don't think they will be pleased to see us!" said the Mayor.

"No, I don't suspect so, but we'll be ready for that!"

"I have no doubt about that, the sheriff trained his deputies well, I'm sure."

"He did Sir!"

"Isn't there children up on that farm?"

"Yes, four of them Sir."

"Just remind your men of that fact deputy. We don't want any children hurt in this!"

"Understood, but isn't that their parent's responsibility, and if they put them in harms way, well Mayor, there wouldn't be much we could do about it!"

"Let's hope that doesn't happen deputy."

The deputy pulled up outside the station. Five other deputies were preparing to leave for the farm. "The Mayor will be taking the place of the sheriff," the deputy told them.

"Mayor," each acknowledging him.

"Right, you all know from before, that these people do not respect the law, and that they are armed! The Mayor would like me to remind you, that there are children on that farm, and that harming them must be avoided, if at all possible! Are we ready?" They all responded that they were set to go. "Good, load up deputies!"

Part 3

The Siege..

Chapter 33

"No one is searching our property again!" said the man introduced to Margaret as Ash. "We have had enough of being accused every time a crime is committed in this town!"

"That's right, they're always pointing the finger at us! And why? Because we simply don't conform to their ordinary, uninspiring way of life!" his wife Pippa added.

"Please, you don't want any trouble!" Margaret urged them, "Just let them question Max, that's all they'll want!"

Willow replied, "Maybe she's right, I mean, that sheriff is dead now.."

Ash interrupted her, "But don't you see, they will believe that Max killed him!"

His wife Pippa added, "He's right Willow, you heard her," she gestured toward Margaret, "Max was the last person to see the sheriff alive!"

Willow replied, "I don't know anymore, I just don't want any trouble., the children and.," she put her arm around Max, "What do you think? If you go with them, will they just question you, and will that be it?"

Max held her close, "I don't believe they'll take my word for it that I had nothing to do with his death. No matter what I tell them, it will not be what they want to hear."

"He's right Willow," said Beth. "What do you think Jodi?"

Jodi, until now, had remained silent, "I think they should question Max here."

Margaret responded, "They won't agree to that!"

Willow answered, "Max is not leaving here with them! They will *have* to agree to that! He has done nothing!"

One by one, all of them agreed that Max was not going with the deputies when they came to take him in for questioning. This was not the outcome Margaret had hoped for. "When they don't agree to this," Margaret knew it was a matter of *when* and not *if*, "what will you all do then?"

Jodi answered, "We will do whatever we have to!"

Margaret asked, "And the children, what about them?"

"They will be safe. No harm will come to them," Max replied.

Willow asked him, "Are you sure?"

"Don't worry, I wouldn't let anything happen to them," he assured her.

Margaret was not so sure they would be safe, "Where are they now, in bed?"

Beth answered, "Yes, upstairs."

"If they come at this hour, they will not be coming quietly!" Margaret told them.

"She's right Max," said Willow.

Margaret heard the sirens in the distance, "They're coming! Please just go with them Max, just answer their questions," she urged him.

"He's going nowhere with them!" Jodi told her.

Margaret knew, that with their sheriff now dead, the deputies would not be so tolerant of them this time round. They were making a huge mistake, and one that may cost them their lives, including that of their children's! The sound of the sirens grew louder. "Wake the children! Get them out of here!" Margaret urged them.

"Okay," said Max, "Get them out of here!"

And Beth, along with Willow and Pippa, went upstairs to get the children. Margaret watched as Max, Jodi and Ash got their shotguns ready. "What are you going to do with them?"

Ash looked at her, "Protect ourselves!"

Margaret realised then, that she may very well be caught up in the middle of a siege!

The sirens were even louder now, they were close, real close! The three women returned from upstairs carrying the four children in their arms. Max looked out of the window, he could see four patrol cars racing toward the farmhouse. "This proves they already believe I'm guilty!" The children rubbed their eyes, none fully awake.

"Get them out of here!" Max told the women.

Willow asked, "Where? Where do we take them?"

Margaret remembered she had parked her car out back, "Take them out the back, put them into my car!"

"What for? How will they be safe there?" Willow asked her.

Max told Margaret, "They're now coming up the drive. You can get them out of here!"

"Me? How? They're coming up the drive!"

"Yes you can, there's a small dirt track, if you go now you won't be seen!" Ash told her. "Just don't turn on your headlamps until you're well out of sight of the farmhouse," he instructed her.

Max urged his wife, and the other women, "Quick! Hurry, take them out the back!"

Margaret helped the three women carry the children to her car. "Any of you coming with me?" Still reluctant to be taking the children with her.

Willow answered, "I'm staying here with Max."

Pippa and Beth both said they *too* were staying. "But the children, they don't even know who I am!" Margaret told them.

Willow kissed the children, "This is Margaret, she will look after you, be good for her, you all hear?"

Margaret could here the tyres of the patrol cars skid as they came to a sudden halt at the front of the farmhouse, "I don't even know their names!"

There were three girls and one boy, and Beth pointed to each of them in turn, "This is Umi," she told Margaret. "Eden," she pointed to the little boy. "Butterfly and Light," she continued, their names representative of their parent's new found culture.

Margaret noted that the youngest, the girl named Umi, could be no more than three years old. The boy, Eden, roughly about five years, and the other two girls, in the region of six and eight years. They called out to their Moms as Margaret got into the car, "Where do I take them?"

Willow answered, "Just keep them with you, we trust you!"

"We know they'll be safe with you," said Beth.

Pippa hugged Margaret, "We know you won't let any harm come to them."

"Of course I wouldn't, but they need to be with their parents, not me!"

They heard shouting coming from the front of the farmhouse, it was the sheriff's deputies. "Hurry!" Beth told Margaret, "There's the track," she pointed, and with the blessings of a full moon, Margaret was able to see the track clearly, "keep on it and you will come to the Myers' farm."

"The Myers' place?"

"Yes, now go!" she urged.

Margaret closed the car door, and watched the three women go back inside the farmhouse. She hoped it would not be the last time she would see them alive!

The children whimpered as Margaret quietly pulled away from the farmhouse. "It's okay," she told them, "you'll all see your Moms and Dads soon," she hoped. She then drove along the dirt track until she came to the Myers' farm, and from there she turned onto the highway, deciding to take the children to Mark's friend, Mel, and his wife. They were good people, and the children, she knew, would be safe with them. However there would be no time to explain the whole situation to Mel, getting back to the farm without delay was imperative!

Now on the highway, Margaret looked in the rear-view mirror, the children had fallen back to sleep. It wasn't long before she arrived at Mel's place.

His was one of six houses that had been built by the Air Force, for the purpose of housing those who wished to live off base, however they were no longer used for this purpose, and had been sold off privately. Margaret had read somewhere that they had not been used by the Air Force for several years. Whatever was going on now at the Air base, was intended to stay.

Margaret knocked on the door, "Mel! Are you in?" She knocked harder, "Mel!"

The light on the porch came on. "Who is it?"

"Mel, it's me Margaret, Mark's friend."

He opened the door, "What are you doing here this time of night? Have you heard from Mark?"

Mel's wife also came to the door, "Who is it Mel?"

"Sorry to wake you Lori," said Margaret. "No, it's not because of Mark that I'm here."

Mel looked toward Margaret's car, "Who are they?"

"That's why I'm here."

"Aren't they the children from the old Duggan's farm?" Lori asked. "Why are they with you?"

"Yes they are, but I really don't have time to explain now. Can I leave them with you both, just for the night?"

Mel asked, "Why? Where are their parents?"

"I wouldn't ask only it's an emergency! I promise I will explain when I get back."

"They don't know us, won't they be frightened?" asked Lori.

"They're very sleepy, put them straight to bed, and I'm sure they will be fine."

"Okay," said Mel, "but I don't know where they will all sleep."

"Two can sleep in the guest room, and the other two can go on the put-you-up in the den," said Lori. "Bring them in. Mel, help her while I get the beds ready."

"Thank you both for this!"

"There better be a good explanation for this," said Mel.

"There is," Margaret answered.

Mel helped her carry the children into the house, and put each of them to bed.

"I'll be back by morning," she told them, "I've got to hurry now!" She got into her car, and drove away, heading back the way she had come, praying she wouldn't be too late!

Turning off the highway at the Myers' farm, and onto the dirt track that led back to the Duggan's farm, Margaret wondered if the deputies had managed to convince Max to go with them for questioning. She didn't believe for a moment, that the deputies would agree to do their questioning of him at the farm. And with all of them determined that Max should not go with the deputies, there could be no other outcome, but a stand-off!

Margaret stopped the car as soon as the farmhouse came into view, deciding to walk the rest of the way, so as not to be heard. Now out of the car, she could hear the shots; gunfire! She was too late!

Chapter 34

The moon was now low in the sky. It cast an eerie glow over the farm. The gunfire raged from both inside and outside of the farmhouse. Margaret kept herself low as she approached the house, not wishing to get hit by a stray bullet! Now only twelve yards or so from the house, she was unable to go any further; the deputies had now surrounded the farmhouse. She could see two deputies laying low on either side of her, and both just a few feet away. They hadn't seen her approach. Margaret retreated a little so as to remain unseen. There was no way she was going to get back inside the farmhouse now!

Shots could be heard coming from the front of the farmhouse, and along with the deputies on either side of her also firing, the sound was terrifying. Margaret attempted to block out the noise by lowering her head, and putting her hands over her ears. A few moments later, the two deputies ceased firing. Margaret looked up, and taking her hands away from her head, she heard them communicate to the deputies at the front of the farmhouse, through hand-held radios. They were talking about using tear gas!

There was a short discussion before it was decided, that one of them would cover the other as he approached the back of the farmhouse with the canisters. Margaret could do nothing, only watch. The deputy crawled along the ground toward the farmhouse. What was going to happen when they came outside? Would the deputies just shoot them? Margaret was filled with dread. With the canisters having been thrown inside the farmhouse, the deputy retreated.

There followed an unearthly silence. Margaret saw a flickering light from inside. There had been no lights on in the farmhouse throughout the gun firing. The light seemed to become brighter. Suddenly there was a loud explosion. It made her ears pop and then sting. She put her hands to them, covering them, attempting to ease the pain. All the while she kept her eyes fixed upon the farmhouse. A fire had ensued, engulfing the small farmhouse, and rapidly, it spread to the roof. Windows blew out, and huge plumes of smoke bellowed out from them. Just seconds later and the smoke plumes became blazing fire flames, shooting out of every window and door. Nobody stirred from inside. No one could survive this inferno! Margaret got to her feet, no longer did she care if she were seen. "Someone help them!" She ran toward the house, "Get them out!" The intensity of the flames held her back, preventing her from getting any where near.

"What are you doing?" shouted one of the deputies. "Get back!"

"For god's sake help them!"

The two deputies approached her, keeping low of the flames, "We can't go in there!" They both took hold of her, pulling her from the blazing farmhouse.

"You can't just let them die in there!"

"You have to stay back, it's not safe," the deputy told her. They took her around to the front of the farmhouse.

"What are you doing here?" asked the Mayor.

Margaret looked back at the burning farmhouse, "Why did you set fire to it?"

"We didn't! And you have no business being here!" he told her.

Margaret yelled, "They didn't do anything!"

"They killed the sheriff and the Myers!" answered the Mayor.

"You don't know that for sure! Where's your evidence? And who's in charge?"

"Look Miss, I don't need to answer any of your questions, and you should not be here, this is police business!"

The farmhouse continued to burn, "Didn't anyone get out?" Margaret realised she was now crying. If they were all dead, what was going to happen to the children?

"I asked who's in charge?"

"I am," the Mayor told her.

"What? Who are you?"

"The Mayor!"

"You're the Mayor?"

"Yes Miss, I am the Mayor, and who may I ask are you?"

"Margaret Baker, I work.."

He didn't let her finish, "I heard about you, the newspaper reporter."

Margaret answered, "That's right," surprised to hear he had heard about her. "Why are you in charge?"

The deputy told her, "With the sheriff now., well he's in charge."

"Thank you deputy, but I can handle this," said the Mayor.

"You gave the order for this?" asked Margaret.

"I told you, we did not set alight to the farmhouse!"

"I know what I saw!"

The deputy grabbed hold of her by the arm, "You shouldn't even be here!"

"It's okay deputy, let her go," said the Mayor.

Margaret pulled free of the deputy's hold. The Mayor and the other deputies stood watching the blaze.

"We caught her trying to get in there," he told the Mayor, as he pointed toward the inferno.

"Why aren't you doing something to help them?"

The deputy added, ignoring her question, "And she seems to think we had something to do with this."

The Mayor looked at her, "I see, so you think we did this Miss?"

"I saw the deputy throw the canisters in there!"

"Tear gas, Miss, just a little encouragement to get them to come out," said the Mayor.

"Well they caused that fire!"

The Mayor turned to one of the deputies, "Can that happen deputy?"

"I don't think so, I've never heard of that happening before," he replied.

"Perhaps they started it themselves Miss," suggested the Mayor.

Margaret replied, "Nonsense! They wouldn't do that, they have children!"

The Mayor asked, "You know the people that own this farm?"

"Did anyone get out?" She asked again, "Why aren't you doing something to help them?"

There was a loud crash, and everyone turned to look at the farmhouse. The roof had collapsed. "There is nothing we can do," the Mayor told her.

"So we just stand here, while innocent people burn to death?"

"What would you suggest we do? It's impossible to get anyway *near* in order to help," he told her. "I'm sorry, but no one can help them now."

Margaret knew it too, but just didn't want to accept it. The children! What was she going to tell them? All of them orphaned on this terrible night!

Chapter 35

No one had survived the blaze. Max, Willow, Beth, Ash, Jodi and Pippa, were now dead; perished in the fire. No one knew what had caused the explosion, and the subsequent fire, but that didn't stop the Mayor, along with the sheriff's deputies, from blaming it on the owners. "That's what they do!" said one of the deputies. "They make a suicide pact!"

Margaret was most irritated by his remark, "What are you talking about? Why would they do that? That's ridiculous!"

"How many were in there deputy?" asked the Mayor.

"Six adults and four children," he replied.

Margaret corrected the deputy, "No there wasn't! The children were not in there!"

The Mayor regarded her with curiosity, "And how do *you* know that?"

"Where are they then?" asked the deputy.

"I took them just before you all arrived."

The Mayor asked, "I'm curious, why would you do that?"

"I knew they wouldn't be safe here!" she turned to look at the burning farmhouse, "And I was right!"

The Mayor asked, "So you spoke to these people before we arrived? So what did you all talk about?"

"I asked if Max had seen what had happened to the sheriff."

The deputy said, "Of course he had, he killed the sheriff!"

She replied, "No he did not, deputy!"

The Mayor inquired, "Who's Max?"

"He's the man the sheriff arrested," she told him.

"The one that had been held in the very same cell the sheriff was found dead in later!"

Margaret was tired of the deputy's unfounded accusations, "Look deputy, he did not kill him. In fact the sheriff had let him go, and was alive when he left!"

The Mayor asked her, "So how did you know the sheriff was dead?"

"Yes, that's right, how did you know?" asked the deputy.

Margaret had no choice but tell them, "I found him."

"You found him? And instead of alerting the deputies, you came out here?" The Mayor regarded her with suspicion, "Why?"

"I just wanted to know if he had seen anyone, or if he was all right."

The Mayor asked, "You didn't think he could have killed the sheriff?"

"No I didn't think for a moment that he had done it!"

"Why not?" The Mayor's distrust now more obvious, "How were you so sure he hadn't killed the sheriff?"

"That's not their way Mayor. They are peace loving people, or were," she glanced back at the *now* unrecognisable farmhouse.

"Or was it because you already *knew* who had killed him?" said the Mayor.

"No, of course not!"

The deputy spoke, "And we still haven't found your friend!"

"Yes., I recall the sheriff mentioning him to me," said the Mayor. "Does he know the people that own this farm?"

"*Owned* you mean," she answered. "You can't own anything when you're dead!"

The Mayor asked, "Where is he, your friend?"

"Probably dead too!" Margaret wanted so much to tell them, if only to stop Mark from being accused of such deplorable crimes, but she couldn't. "All I know is that Mark is gone., missing, and now these people are dead! If there are any more killings, who will be accused next?"

"You! Perhaps you were involved!" said the deputy.

"Me? Are you completely crazy?"

"Well you found the Myers, and the sheriff! And you were here when that fire started!"

"The deputy is right, you have been present throughout all these incidents," said the Mayor. "And since you arrived to this town, those crop patterns began to appear too! What have you got to say about that?"

"I have nothing to say Mayor, as no one would listen anyway!"

"Maybe we should bring you in, and hold you for questioning," said the deputy.

Margaret held out her arms, putting her hands together, "Here put the cuffs on then!"

The deputy reached for his handcuffs, "Fine.,"

The Mayor stopped him, "Leave it deputy."

"No it's fine, let him, I've nothing to hide!"

"Don't push our patience Miss. Why don't you just go now, and leave the deputies to get on with their job. Where did you take the children?"

"They're safe. They're with a friend nearby."

"What friend?" asked the deputy.

"Not Mark, if that's what you're thinking!"

The Mayor said, "Just tell us who?"

"Mel and his wife."

"Okay, well they can't stay there," he told her.

"They are fine there for the moment Mayor, I mean, where would you take them?"

Margaret needed to get back to Mel's before morning, and before the children woke up looking for their parents. The Mayor was of no help whatsoever, having only suggested sending a deputy to have the children taken straight to the child welfare authorities. Margaret suggested they try and find any relatives of the children's parents, let them know the situation, and perhaps they would take them in instead. It had taken much persuasion to convince the Mayor that this was best for the children.

"As long as they agree to look after them until any relatives can be traced," the Mayor told her.

"They will Mayor," she assured him. Now all she had to do was convince Mel and his wife. It was almost dawn as Margaret hurriedly made her way back to Mel's.

Chapter 36

All was still when Margaret arrived at Mel's house. Dawn was now breaking, and the moon was no where to be seen. She walked up to the front door, and could see instantly that something was not quite right. The front door was open, and a small child's blanket lay on the ground. She recognised it at once, it belonged to the youngest of the children. *What was it doing there?*

"Hello., Mel, Lori, are you there?" Margaret picked up the child's blanket, "Mel, it's Margaret," slowly she pushed open the front door and stepped inside, "Mel, are you there?" She was greeted only by silence. "Mel! Where are you?"

All kinds of frightening images came to mind, and she was reluctant to go into the house. Would she find Mel, Lori and the children brutally mutilated? How many more would be killed this night? She stood in the hallway, unable to move. "Mel are you all right?" the silence only helped confirm that all was not well. She prayed that she would not discover another horrific scene of butchery, and within one of the rooms of the now dark, and eerily still house.

Perhaps the Mayor had lied to her, and had sent a deputy ahead, to remove the children before she got there? But if that were true, then where was Mel and his wife? Margaret, and against her better judgement, entered the family den, where two of the children had been put to bed. "Lori, are you in here?" She wasn't, and neither were the children. Margaret searched the rest of the house, but found no one.

Where had they gone? Margaret searched the house, frantically looking for some clue as to where they could have gone. In the kitchen, and in an open drawer, were a pile of sketches, which she recognised at once. They were of the crop patterns, and most probably the same sketches that Mark had given Mel to decipher!

Margaret took them out of the drawer to take a closer look at them. The first two she recalled Mark showing her, but the rest she had not seen before. They looked different from Mark's somehow. The sketch Mark had spoke of, the one that displayed symbols giving directions to the Air base in the desert, was among the pile. Margaret also found a small hand written note among them, it read;

The sheriff called today, asked if I had seen your friend Mark, I said I hadn't. I told the sheriff about those sketches he gave you. I showed him the one that gave directions to a command centre in the desert, and said that he may have gone out there to check it out. Your dinner is in the oven. Don't wait up for me as I'll be back late. Dad is not having a good day.

Love you
Lori.

The sheriff knew where Mark had gone all along! Why had he not said anything? And why then, did he think Mark was hiding somewhere on the old Duggan's farm? The sheriff had known Mark was out in the desert, so why get a warrant to search Max's farm? Who did he believe was committing these brutal murders? Margaret's head was reeling. She needed time to think; clear her mind. But now Mel, Lori and the children were missing! *What the hell was going on?* Margaret took the note and the sketches, and headed for the sheriff's office, where she was sure she would find Mel, Lori *and* the children.

Chapter 37

Bram waited for the lieutenant to transport him from his quarters to the mountain facility. His assignment that day, he had been informed, was to assist the scientists with their gravitational-force testing on the human body, by flight simulation. These tests would, most likely, involve him flying one of the alien crafts stored in the mountain facility.

Bram observed the jeep pull up outside, and was surprised to see that it was not the lieutenant driving, but the Colonel instead. He wondered why the Colonel himself had come for him. He went to meet him, "Good morning Sir."

"Morning lieutenant, get in," the Colonel instructed Bram. "Going to be an interesting day, I'm sure." The Colonel turned the jeep in the direction of the mountain, "Looking forward to seeing your flight endurance skills."

Bram looked puzzled, "My flight endurance skills Sir?"

"Don't worry, just do what you always do lieutenant," the Colonel expressed his amusement.

"Am I to fly one of those alien crafts Sir?"

"You're quick, I'll give you that!"

"So I am to fly them?" Bram was not at all impressed by the Colonel's wise cracks.

The Colonel became conscious of this, "Sorry lieutenant, I'm just in a good mood today. I don't get many great days, but today is certainly one of them. To answer your question; yes, you will be test flying them."

"Them?"

"Yes, *them* lieutenant," the Colonel more serious now, "We know the crafts still operate, and we have seen their manoeuvrability, but as yet, no human has flown them. That's where you come in."

Bram asked, "Are they safe to fly?"

"Well if you mean, do they have an ejection seat should anything go wrong, then no, they don't! But don't worry, they've crash landed before and no one died."

"But you said no human has flown them before?"

The Colonel looked at Bram, "When I said no one, I didn't mean human lieutenant."

"Oh right," Bram loved to fly any aircraft, but the thought of an alien craft left him feeling quite anxious, "What makes you think I could operate any of them?"

"You were posted here because of your unique flying skills lieutenant, not every pilot has the natural abilities you have."

Bram understood himself to be quite an accomplished pilot, as even back at the training academy his skills had surpassed all others, including his instructors. "I will do my best Sir."

They arrived at the mountain facility, "I have no doubt you will lieutenant," answered the Colonel.

Chapter 38

There was a lot of activity at the sheriff's office. It was barely 7am, Margaret had had no sleep the night before, and she was now beginning to feel the affects of it. Along with this, and the tangled events of the previous night, Margaret was quite unable to bring together, all what had occurred over the few past days. The Mayor stood by the sheriff's desk surrounded by four deputies.

"Where's Mel and his wife?"

They all turned to look at her. "Miss Baker." The Mayor asked, "do you mean the couple you took the children to?"

"Yes. Where are they?"

The Mayor approached her, "I assume they are at their home," he regarded her curiously, "Aren't they?"

Margaret looked around at the deputies, "Didn't you send one of them to bring them here?"

"No I did not," the Mayor replied.

"They were not at their home," Margaret had until now managed to suppress her worst fears, that they had not been taken to the sheriff's office after all, "When I got there, they were gone!"

"What?" the Mayor along with the deputies gathered round her, "Gone where?"

"I don't know!"

"You took them there," the Mayor now expressing his displeasure, "You had better find them!"

Margaret was taken aback by the Mayor's words, "Find them? Me? Why?"

The Mayor instructed the deputies to go to Mel's house and check it out, "And look for anything that may give us some idea as to where they've got to!"

"There was nothing, I checked," Margaret told him. There was one thing though; a note. It revealed the sheriff had known Mark had gone out to the desert Air base.

The Mayor asked, "You checked? Are you now a police officer Miss Baker?"

"I was only seeing if there.."

The Mayor interrupted her, "You seem to be in *all* the places, at *all* the wrong times, is that merely coincidence?"

"I don't know what you're trying to say Mayor, but I can assure you.."

Again he interrupted, "The facts are, that since you arrived, along with your friend and those hippies, things around here have taken a turn for the worst. You can't deny that Miss Baker!"

Margaret was not about to allow herself be accused of everything that had occurred in the back-water town, "I had nothing to do with any killings, and neither did Mark! Those *hippies* as you refer to them, did nothing either!"

"You know that? How?"

"Well we'll never know now, will we Mayor?"

"What do you mean?"

"I mean, as *now* they are all dead!"

"Your friend is still out there somewhere," the Mayor replied.

"He's.," Margaret almost blurted it out, "He's.,"

"He's what?"

"Innocent!"

"What I want to know is, has he contacted you?"

"No, he has not Mayor," Margaret wanted to end the conversation regarding Mark, "What caused the fire?"

"Is this for the newspaper Miss Baker?"

She was beginning to dislike the Mayor just as much as she had the sheriff, "Yes, it is," she asserted, but that was a lie.

"A faulty tear gas canister," he told her.

"But didn't one of the deputies say that it would be unlikely, as he hadn't heard.."

"Look, that was the cause," the Mayor was clearly irritated, "Unlikely, yes, but it *was* the cause of the fire!"

"How can you know so soon, and for certain?"

"We just do, and it is not for you to know the full details of police investigations, is it Miss Baker?"

"I wasn't trying.."

"I know how you are, the sheriff told me all about your meddling in police business."

"I wasn't interfering Mayor."

"Whatever, but I have a job to do, and would appreciate it if you kept out of my way and of my deputies' too."

Margaret had no intention of being in his company if she could at all help it, "I will."

"Then we'll get along just fine, I'm sure," said the Mayor.

Margaret on the other hand didn't agree, "Yes well, we now have ten, I mean nine people dead, and one missing.."

"Seven missing," the Mayor corrected.

"Oh yes of course, Mel, his wife and the four children," she had been including Mark in the number of the dead, "Yes seven missing."

"And your point is?"

"What?" asked Margaret.

"You were saying that there are nine people dead, and?"

"Seven are missing, and strange patterns in wheat fields," Margaret answered.

"No one cares about crop patterns! And neither do I."

"But they must be linked somehow!"

"Look, I don't think we have anything further to say, for now, so if you don't mind, I've got work to do," the Mayor motioned her to the door, "If we need to speak to you, we will let you know, so don't go disappearing like your friend did."

"I have no intention of going anywhere Mayor," she lied, already deciding to return to the Air base, but only after she had done a little investigating of her own. The newspaper archives would be a good place to start, and subsequently, she would return to the Air base.

Chapter 39

The seat was a little tight. He had been informed to expect the interior to be *compact*, but *small* would have been a better description, for there was only ample room inside for a child! Nevertheless, Bram done as instructed and squeezed himself into the tiny pilot seat. There was no belt to secure himself with, although if there had been, he doubted it would have fitted across him. The interior was all dark grey in colour. The windscreen was made up of a single portion, of a type of darkened glass he had never seen before. It provided the pilot with an all round visual in front, and on both sides of the craft. With his helmet on securely, Bram now spoke to ground control through its inbuilt mike system, "How does this thing start up?"

"We don't know exactly," came the response.

Just like the description of the interior given, he expected the true answer was, that they had no idea whatsoever!

"Right, so what do you suggest I try?"

"Just whatever comes to mind."

What the hell did that mean? Whatever comes to mind? He'd never been in an alien craft before, how could he possibly even guess how it operated? "You've got to give me something!"

The voice through his helmet, "Just try touching or turning some switches."

"There are no switches, just a shiny black surface around me, like a desk!" Bram reached out and touched it. As soon as he had, a sound came from the back of his seat, "Wait, something's happening!" The already small seat began to tighten around him, "What the hell!" He tried to move but was unable to.

"What's going on lieutenant?"

Bram answered, "The seat seems to be alive, and it's moulding itself around me!"

"Relax lieutenant," it was the Colonel this time, "Just go with it."

Bram, although uneasily so, did as the Colonel instructed. The seat continued to shape itself around him, "Okay it's stopped now, I'm fine," said Bram. The seat was now a perfect fit, "This is unbelievable!"

The Colonel spoke to him again through his helmet, "Calm yourself lieutenant, you're not finished yet, you still need to get off the ground!"

How on earth was he going to do that? There was no control panel, no switches, nothing! "I don't know how I'm going to operate this thing Sir."

"Whatever you did to get that seat moving, do it again!"

"I didn't do anything, just touched the.." Bram pressed his fingers against the black shiny surface, he now referred to as a desk. At that moment, there came a loud whooshing sound, "What's that?" he removed his hands from the surface of the desk.

"It would seem you have managed to get it operating lieutenant," said the Colonel.

"I have?"

"Yes, now would you care to give it a test flight lieutenant?"

Bram knew the Colonel would not accept no for an answer, "Yes Sir, I'll try Sir."

"Good lieutenant, whenever you're ready."

Bram realised the alien craft was still inside the mountain, "How do I manoeuvre it out of the facility?"

"I'm sure you'll manage it lieutenant," the Colonel answered. "I have every faith in you."

He did? Why? "Yes Sir," Bram replied. Again he moved his finger tips across the black surface, it felt cold but somehow alive. "Nothing is happening Sir."

"On the contrary, you have lifted the craft off the ground by at least ten metres," said the Colonel. "You're doing just fine."

He had? Bram had felt nothing, no movement whatsoever. "It doesn't feel like the craft is moving at all!"

The Colonel instructed him to use visual, and with no instruments to work with, there really wasn't much else for Bram to go on!

"I have a visual on the facility opening Sir," Bram kept his finger tips pressed against the black surface. He had no idea how he was operating the alien craft, "It seems to be responding to touch Sir."

"What do you mean lieutenant?"

"I have my finger tips pressed against the surface of the desk in front of me, it seems to me to be some kind of control panel, but without any switches! Perhaps they are below the surface, and by pressing down, they respond?" It was all guesswork at that point and Bram knew it.

"Well whatever you're doing lieutenant, keep doing it!"

The craft was nearing the opening now, "What happens when I get outside Sir?"

"We'll worry about that when you get it outside," replied the Colonel.

Bram worried about it at that moment, "Sir?"

"You will be fine lieutenant."

The craft passed through the opening and was now outside of the mountain facility, on the other side of the mountain range, and hidden from the Air base. Nothing ahead of Bram now but clear skies above and empty desert below. He kept a visual as the craft increased speed. "I have no idea what speed this thing is doing Sir, but the ground below is now just a blur and I still feel like the craft is not moving at all!" At this speed, whatever that was exactly, Bram expected to be pressed back into his seat, but he felt absolutely nothing! Even he was more surprised when the Colonel informed him that the alien craft was now flying supersonically!

"Did I hear you correct Sir? Supersonic speed?"

"Yes lieutenant, we have an F-102 on your tail," the Colonel told him.

"Oh right," Bram was now beginning to understand why the F-102 was required on the Air base, "May I return Sir?" Bram no longer wanted to continue flying the alien craft, "I have no thought as to how, but I would like to return to the facility, Sir."

"You may return lieutenant whenever you're ready."

The alien craft slowed, it turned back in the direction of the mountain facility, and picked up speed once more. "It seems to be doing it all by itself Sir!"

"You're doing very well lieutenant."

"I'm not really doing anything Sir." Back through the opening, Bram could now see the empty space where the alien craft had been moments before. The craft landed on the same exact spot. Bram removed his hands from the shiny black surfaced desk. The seat released him. He was happy to be disembarking from the unearthly craft.

"Well done lieutenant, knew you wouldn't let us down," said the Colonel.

"Thank you Sir, but I don't think it was me doing the flying!"

"Nonsense lieutenant, you were the only one up there," the Colonel was certainly in high spirits. "Very pleased, that's the first time we've seen that craft in action!"

"It was? But how did it get here?"

"Oh don't worry about that now, there's a lot to do," said the Colonel. "I want you to talk with these scientists, and explain to them what you just did in there."

Bram wasn't sure what, or *if* he had done anything, still convinced the alien craft had been *somehow* in control all along!

Part 4

The Return..

Chapter 40

In the basement of the newspaper office, and now searching through the microfilm data, wherein all the newspaper's archives were stored, Margaret felt confident she would unearth some reference to the Air base in past articles. The houses in the town, one of which Mel and Lori lived, had been built for the purpose of providing homes to Air Force service men, and their families, who wished to live off the Air base. The houses, she had been informed by her boss when she had first arrived to the town, had been constructed some thirty years earlier, in the early 1930's. Margaret concentrated her search on the years between 1930-'33. There was quite a lot to get through. She checked the time; almost 8am. She had a least another hour before her boss showed up.

There it was! An article regarding the construction of the houses; they were completed in January 1930. She read the article; Air base service men and their families first moved in, in February of that year. There were some names too, she was in luck! The names of the first Air men to occupy the houses, one of which struck her immediately, a Sergeant Dan Howard, where had she heard that name before? And there was another, *Stephenson*, Mark's friend was Mel Stephenson! She searched on, looking for anything further on the houses and their occupants.

Many Air men and their families had resided in the houses, but not staying for more than a few months at a time. This was not unusual, as service men could have their postings changed at any point. It all depended on what their skills were, and if the Air base required that skill at that moment in time, if not, they were moved on. Families of the service men lived in the houses up until 1948, when they were then sold off privately.

There was not much more about the houses, so Margaret moved on to the years between 1934 to 1948, when the houses were sold; she found nothing.

She could find no information regarding the desert Air base, other than its commander was a Colonel Maxwell, and was made commander of the Air base in 1930, the same year the houses in the town had been constructed, she noted. Thirty one years on, and he was still in command of the Air base!

Was he the one that was responsible for the death of Mark? She believed he was! And she wanted to know more about this Colonel Maxwell. Margaret was unable to find anything more. She checked the time again, it was almost 9am. Her boss and the other reporters would be arriving soon. She quickly jotted down the names of those that had occupied the houses during the time they were owned by the Air Force, switched off the microfilm data reader, and left the basement.

"Good morning Margaret," her boss had already arrived.

"Morning," she replied.

"Looking for anything in particular, were you?"

Margaret closed the basement door behind her, "Oh, not really."

"I guess you've heard the terrible news about our sheriff and the people.."

Margaret interrupted him, not wishing to get into any discussion with him, "Yes I have. Got someone I need to see right now. Will talk to you later," she headed for the door.

"What about that story?"

She turned to look at him, "What story?"

"The interview you had with those hippies. Now they are dead, I don't see the harm in printing what they had to say!"

Straight away Margaret became infuriated by his statement, but thought it best, for the time being, to say nothing. She just wanted to get back to the Air base, and fast!

"I'll have it for you later, I promise," and she left the office, not waiting for his reply.

Margaret had one more place to go before she would return to the Air base.

Chapter 41

"What you just did up there, well no one else could have done it, I know that," said the Colonel. "I have waited a long time to see that."

"But I really didn't do anything Sir," Bram told him.

"You got that thing to fly lieutenant," he pointed to the alien craft, "Amazing stuff!"

Bram felt like a child being praised for something he hadn't done; he felt insincere.

"I really.."

The Colonel didn't let him finish, "These gentlemen would like you to explain what you just did up there." Three men, approximately the same age as the Colonel, somewhere in their sixties, Bram guessed, and all wearing white coats, stood gazing at the alien craft. "This is lieutenant Howard, he will explain to you what he just did up there," the Colonel told them. None of them spoke, just nodded. "Oh, one other thing lieutenant, we will need to run some tests first."

"Tests?"

"Nothing to worry about, it's just a medical check that's all."

"Why will I need a medical?" The scientists remained silent. "I had one before being posted here." They studied him intently. "I don't see how it's necessary to have another." Their gaze made him feel extremely uncomfortable. "I really.."

"Relax lieutenant, it will be brief, just a simple blood test. We need to be sure all of our pilots are in tip top condition."

The scientists continued to stare. "I feel fine Sir."

"Then you have nothing to worry about. Go with these gentlemen, it won't take long."

Bram had to obey the orders of his commanding officer, but somehow, and for some reason unknown to him, he didn't wish to go with the scientists!

"Is this so necessary Sir?"

The Colonel's demeanour changed, although only slightly, Bram was still aware of it.

"Look lieutenant, for all we know you could have been exposed to high levels of radiation while flying that craft."

"Radiation? Why was I not briefed beforehand about the risks involved?"

"What do you think that thing runs on lieutenant? Aviation fuel?"

"I hadn't thought about it Sir."

"There are no gas stations that we know of, scattered out there in space!"

Bram was not enjoying the Colonel's wise cracks, "I just didn't think about it Sir." He didn't much like the Colonel anyway.

"You will go with theses gentlemen lieutenant, and I will see you back here when you're done," the Colonel walked away, leaving Bram with the three scientists.

"This way lieutenant," one of them said.

Bram went with them.

Chapter 42

Only five, of the usual six men, assembled for the meeting. The venue, unchanged, and the topics for discussion, rarely altered. "Do we know if *everyone* is where we had expected them to be by this time?" one of them asked.

"I understand, and from what I hear from our honourable member, who can not be here this morning, that it's close to that point," another informed him.

"Good, we don't want this dragged out any longer, do we gentlemen?"

They all nodded in agreement. They gathered around the large oval table.

The same man spoke again, "Has our honourable member *confirmed* the success of the project as yet?" he asked.

"Yes he has. It has been established by the subjects themselves," came the response.

"Even better," said another of the men. "My ardent desire has been granted."

"It certainly has," another agreed. "I must confess, that I did think it to be unwise at the time, however, I am happy to be wrong on this occasion."

"Here, here," they all agreed.

Another inquired, "Are we to wait until he returns, before we proceed any further?" They each held equal status; no one man had greater power than the other.

Another responded, "Yes, I think that would be the prudent thing to do. Are we all in agreement?"

"Yes," they all agreed.

Another declared, "I must say, this *is* a joyous occasion."

"Indeed it is!" the others agreed.

"But we must exercise caution, as none of our subjects must ever leave the controlled environment arranged for them. The outside world must never know of their existence," warned another.

"That *too* is being dealt with as we speak gentlemen," answered another man.

"That is good to hear, but it must be guaranteed!"

"It will be, I have been assured of it," he answered.

"I think we should reconvene when our honourable gentleman returns," he added.

They all agreed, and after shaking hands with one another, they left the meeting room.

Chapter 43

The children sat huddled together. They looked lost, and very frightened. Two scientists stood over them. "What's going on? Why are those children here?"

The four children looked at him. They were pale and sickly in appearance. Elliot asked again, "What are they doing here?"

One of the scientists answered, "We are not going to hurt them."

"Why did you say that? I didn't ask you that!" The children stared at Elliot. "I asked why they are here?"

"To help us with our work," he told Elliot.

"What? You can't be serious," Elliot had witnessed their experiments, "they're only children!"

"Like I said, we will not harm them."

Elliot didn't believe him, "Why experiment on children?"

"These children will help us understand," the scientist told him.

"Understand what? Where are their parents? Won't they be looking for them?"

The children didn't take their eyes off him. "I mean, *she* can't be more than three years old," he pointed to one of the children.

"They have no parents. They belong here," the scientist said coldly.

Elliot approached the children, "Where are your parents?"

"Move away sergeant. You are not to speak to them!"

Elliot wanted to hit the scientist, take the children and get them off the base, "Why not?" he knew, however, that he wouldn't get very far. "How can it harm?"

"They don't need your affection," he answered, "You will only make it worse for them."

"What the hell do you mean? How can it be any worse for them?"

"Are you all right, sergeant?"

Elliot turned to see the Colonel standing in the doorway, "Yes Sir., I mean, no.."

The Colonel walked toward him, and looked at the children, "Perhaps you should have been briefed first?" He turned and looked back at the doorway, "Lieutenant!"

The lieutenant entered the room.

"Yes Sir?"

"Why was sergeant Dayton not briefed this morning?"

"I don't know Sir."

The Colonel looked at Elliot, "Well, not to mind, I'll brief him now." He turned his attention to the children, "No need to be afraid, no harm will come to you here," he told them. Their eyes remained fixed on Elliot. He couldn't help but notice how blue they were, they seemed to shimmer. They all had blonde hair, and looked quite similar. Most probably siblings. Three girls and one boy, Elliot noted.

"Where did they come from?" Elliot asked.

"They have no family now. We will be taking care of them," the Colonel replied.

"What happened to them?"

"No one really knows. But they will be safe with us."

"An Air base is no place for children."

"Why is that sergeant?"

"They will need schooling, and other children to play with.."

The Colonel interrupted him, "They will get all the knowledge they need here, and as for playing, it's a big base sergeant, lots of space for them to play and run around."

"I think you're mad Colonel!" it was too late, he had said it, and he couldn't take it back.

"What sergeant? You think I'm mad?" he laughed loudly, "I forgot to mention, their parents may be dead, but they have some relatives sergeant."

The children looked at the Colonel, but said nothing. "I see, so they will help look after them?"

"That's the plan!"

"I see."

"So you see sergeant, I am not about to let anything happen to them, am I?"

"No, I guess not Sir," Elliot was not so sure the Colonel was being totally honest.

"We will need their assistance with some projects, but no harm will come to them, I can assure you of that. Understood?"

"Yes Sir, understood."

The Colonel ushered the scientists to take the children, and to make sure they got something to eat. "Let us finish up for the day and resume back here tomorrow," the Colonel told Elliot. "Let's say, 0600hrs."

Elliot watched as the scientists took the children from the room, "Yes Sir," he answered.

"The lieutenant here will escort you from the building," said the Colonel. "And I will remind you sergeant, you do not discuss this with anyone."

"No Sir, I won't," he lied.

Chapter 44

The town hall was situated opposite the sheriff's office, and it was a hive of activity. The Mayor was there, as was Tom Myers. Neither of the men saw Margaret slip through the crowd. People were clearly angry, and the Mayor was trying to calm the situation. Now in the storeroom, where all the records of the town's citizens were kept. Margaret searched among them, particularly looking out for the name *Stephenson*; Dan Stephenson.

The door had been left unlocked, the person in charge most probably having left abruptly upon hearing the commotion outside. She wouldn't have long, the person would return shortly, having become conscious of their oversight. She found Myers; the marriage record of Frank and Harriett Myers. Looking at the date, Margaret was able to see that they had been married for almost thirty years, and that Harriett's name before the marriage had been, *Harriett Thomas*. They both had been born and raised in the town. That was all Margaret could find, which was unusual as they had a son; Tom. She searched through the records and found no mention of the Myers ever having children. How strange, she thought. She could think of no explanation for there being no record, other than, they had had *no* children!

Time was running out, she needed to check the name Stephenson. She found it; Dan Stephenson, an Air man. Now she needed to check if he and his wife had ever had any children. She found the record of their marriage, but nothing else. Just like the Myers, there was no record of any births to the couple either! What was going on? She knew they had a son, *Mel*, but there was no record of him! She also knew the Myers had a son, however, there was no record of him either. Perhaps there was a simple explanation for the lack of any birth records. Maybe they had been born in another state?

Margaret heard someone coming. She quickly replaced everything and slipped out of the room, and just in time. How the approaching woman hadn't seen her, she'll never know. She still had more questions than answers, and this only lending to frustrate her more. One thing she did know for sure, was that Colonel Maxwell was very much in command of the Air base, and had been for well over thirty years! She wanted him to pay for the death of her friend, but *how* she would do this, she still had no thought.

Again she passed through the crowd without been seen by the Mayor. Tom Myers was now, nowhere to be seen. "Quiet! One at a time please," the Mayor shouted to the crowd. "The people responsible for these brutal killings will no longer be able to kill again, I can assure you all of that!"

That statement confirmed it; the Mayor, along with law enforcement, believed that Max and the others had been responsible for the killings! This infuriated Margaret, but there was not a lot she could do about it, and she had to get back to the Air base. Back there she might be able to find out a little more about Mel's father, sergeant Stephenson, and perhaps get a clue as to where Mel and Lori had got to.

The children! Where were the children? She sought to find them also. Mel and Lori wouldn't have just took off with them? She had wanted to help trace the children's relatives, but without their parent's full names, it would be impossible. She only knew them by their first names. And by the look of the situation back at the town hall, neither the Mayor, nor the police, were doing anything to find them! Margaret got into her car, and started out toward the desert.

Chapter 45

Bram had finished for the day, having only flown one of the alien crafts. The tests had come back clear of radiation exposure, and he was relieved about that. How he had succeeded in operating the craft, he couldn't guess, but flown it he had. He looked at his hands, all he had done was touch the surface of..

"Oh you're here."

Bram swung round to see Elliot standing by the doorway of the living room. "How did you get in here?" He was shocked to see him standing there.

"Something wrong with your hands?"

Bram realised he was still holding them up in front of him, "I asked you, how you got in here?" He put his hands down, and ignored Elliot's question.

Elliot pointed to where he had come, "Through the open window in the hallway."

"Why?" Bram was incensed at Elliot's impromptus visit.

"Didn't think you'd be here. Thought it unwise at this time of day to be hanging round your front door!"

Bram approached him, "Well you can go back the way you came, I'm in no mood.."

"I had to come," Elliot interrupted, "There are children here!"

"Children? Where?"

"Here, on the base!"

"So, what if there are, what do you want me to do about it?"

Elliot thought for a moment, then asked, "Where do you suppose they came from?"

"Why are you bothering me with all this?" said Bram angrily, unable to hide his irritation.

Elliot paid no attention to Bram's obvious bad mood, "The Colonel said they belong to him now, whatever that means."

Bram asked, "They belong to him?" now showing a little more interest in what Elliot had to say. "Who told you that?"

"He did!"

"The Colonel has children?"

Elliot went to the sofa and sat down, "No, they're not his exactly, well they are now."

"Will you be clear!"

"Yes. Sorry," Elliot took a moment.

Bram remained standing, "Just tell me what the Colonel told you."

"He said that their parents were dead, and as he was their only relative, they now belong to him."

Bram asked, "And he used that word, *belong?*"

"Yes."

"I see," said Bram.

Elliot regarded him curiously, "Why should that word be so significant to you?"

"No reason really, just thought.."

"Thought what?"

"Nothing, and you can't stay here, you have to go," Bram told him.

"I can't go now, it's still daylight!"

"That's your problem! You got here in daylight, didn't you?"

Elliot stood up, "I'm staying until dusk, so you will just have to put up with my company!"

"Whatever. Do what you want," Bram walked to the hall doorway, darkness would come soon, and he would be left to his own concerns. So what if the Colonel was now guardian of some kids, it wouldn't change his plans.

"You making coffee?" Bram did not answer him, and went to the kitchen. Elliot followed, "So what do you think?"

"About the children? Maybe they *are* related to him," Bram answered.

"He plans on raising them here, on the base," Elliot told him.

"Hmm., I see," Bram filled the kettle and put it on the stove.

Elliot got the coffee jar from one of the cupboards, "I just don't trust him."

"Why not?"

"That's a curious question to ask!"

"*Why* is it?"

"Well for a start, look what happened to Margaret's friend!"

Bram asked, "So you know for certain that the Colonel gave the order?"

"Yes, I do! And as it happens, he also plans on using those kids to assist in his experiments!"

"Now how do you know that?"

"He told me!"

"What experiments are they then?"

Elliot replied, "He didn't say exactly."

The kettle began to boil, "If they are related to him, then I don't believe he will allow any harm to come to them," Bram poured the boiling water into the coffee pot.

"That's it you see, I don't believe they are!"

Bram walked back to the living room, carrying the coffee pot. Elliot followed with the cups, "I'm sure he was lying. The children were afraid, and they didn't speak to him."

"Trauma," said Bram.

"Trauma?"

"Yes, trauma. Maybe that's all it was. You said they had just lost their parents."

"Possibly," Elliot considered.

"As soon as daylight wanes, I want you out of here," Bram told him, "Do you understand?"

Chapter 46

Margaret needed to stop and walk the rest of the way. She found a secluded place to leave her car. It was well off the highway, but nowhere near the restricted area of the Air base. It would be a long walk to the mountain, she had come prepared. She reached for the water in the back seat, Tom Myers grabbed hold of her arm. He had been hiding there all along, "What are you doing?" she shouted to him, "Let go of me!" She struggled to get free of his grip but was unable to.

"You! You've known where he was all along!"

"What the hell are you talking about? Let me go!"

He opened the rear door with one hand, making sure to keep a tight hold of her with the other. "You're not going anywhere!" Out of the car now, but still holding on to her, he opened the driver's door. "No point in struggling, I am not about to let you go anywhere!" He reached around the door, and pulled her from the car.

"You're hurting me! Let me go!"

"Hurting you? Not yet I haven't!" He shoved her to the ground.

Margaret tried to get to her feet, "Why are you doing this?"

"I want you to tell me where your friend is hiding!"

She managed to get to her feet, "He's not hiding, he's dead!" She couldn't keep it to herself any longer, "Yes, Mark's dead!"

He regarded her with suspicion, "Dead? I don't believe you!"

"It's true, he's dead!"

"How? When?"

She brushed the dust from her face, and clothes, "A few days ago, on that Air base," she pointed toward the mountain. "So he couldn't have killed the sheriff!"

"But he could have killed my parents!"

"No, he didn't! The sheriff was murdered in the same way, and by the same killer!"

He approached her, "You know who the killer is then?" He went to reach for her, but she was gone! "What the hell!" he spun around, searching for her, "Where.."

"I'm telling you all I know!" she told him.

He looked back at where she had been a split second before. "How did you do that?"

"What?" she asked.

"You were gone just now!" He rubbed at his eyes.

Margaret had no idea what he was talking about, "No I wasn't!"

"You just disappeared!"

"Disappeared? Are you all right?"

"I know what I saw! Or rather what I didn't see!"

"I never moved from this spot, it was probably the dust," she wanted to get away.

"Look it's going to be dark soon, and I have to get back to that Air base," she told him. "You can take my car back to town, if you want to."

"I'm not letting you out of my sight!" he told her. "And what is to stop me from beating the truth out of you?"

"I don't believe for a minute that you are that sort of person!"

Tom replied, "I'm going with you!"

She shook her head, "It's not safe to come with me. They already killed my friend."

"I don't care, I'm going with you!"

Margaret replied, "Fine, but if you don't want to be caught, you had better do as I say!" She went back to the car, and grabbed the water from the backseat.

"I can take care of myself, I *have* just returned from *'Nam*!"

"I'm aware of that," she started out toward the mountains.

Tom followed close behind, "Why do you want to go to that base?"

"I knew you were a good person," she smiled at him.

"Hmm., I wouldn't be so sure of that," he answered.

"Mark came out here looking for some answers to those crop patterns found in your parent's wheat field. He was caught trying to get onto the base. They killed him," she didn't wish to go into the details of his death.

"I'm in the military, and I've never heard of anyone being killed for trespassing on government property! He isn't Russian is he?"

"Don't be ridiculous! And this is no ordinary Air base!"

Tom asked, "How is that?"

"You'll see," she told him. "Were you born in another state?" Margaret had found no record of his parents ever having had a child.

"No. I was born on our farm. Why do you ask?"

"Really, on the farm you say?"

"Yes, that's what I said."

Now that was strange, "I was looking through the town's birth records, and did not find any record of you," she told him.

"So that's why you were at the town hall!"

"You saw me then?"

"Yes. On your way out, you stopped to listen to what the Mayor was saying, so I slipped into your car. You ought not to leave your car open."

"I won't in future!"

"How far more is it to the Air base?"

"Oh about two miles or so," she passed him the water bottle, "Want some?"

"No thanks, I'm fine for now."

She drank some, "So any idea why there should be no record of your birth?"

"None," he answered, "Any idea who the killer is?"

"Well the Mayor reckons it was Max and the others."

"Yes he does, as does the rest of the town," he replied.

"Indeed."

"But you don't think so, do you?"

That was one thing she was sure of, they had nothing to do with the killings. "I have no proof of that, but I'm still certain they didn't kill anyone!"

Tom replied, "That won't change the Mayor's mind!"

"I'm fully aware of that!"

They walked the rest of the way without saying much more to one another. Margaret had no thought as to what she was going to say to Bram and Elliot, about bringing another person onto the base. However, Tom was not about to go away, being adamant that he was going with her. Perhaps that was not a bad thing, as they may need all the help they can get!

Chapter 47

"That's where we need to go," Margaret told him.

"What? Over that mountain?"

"Not over it, through it!"

Tom studied the mountain, "Through it, how?" It was becoming difficult to see very far as it was now getting dark.

"First we need to get close to the base of the mountain, without being seen!"

"By who?"

"There are regular patrols carried out on this side of the mountain," she told him.

"Air base police?"

"Yes, that's right," she looked at him.

"I'm in the military, remember!"

"Then you know what they are like."

"Yes I do!"

They were close to the base of the mountain, "Why that particular one?"

"It's been hollowed out."

"Hollowed out? For what?"

"To hide what they are doing," she told him.

"From the Russians!"

Margaret replied, "From everyone!" She asked, "What time do you make it?"

He looked at his watch, "It's 19.05hrs."

She remembered he was in the military, "Okay, should be fine."

"How do we get in?"

"Just a little further there is an opening. It's used to fly crafts out of."

"They keep aircrafts inside the mountain?"

"I said crafts, I didn't say aircrafts," she told him.

Tom regarded her curiously, "What other craft is there?"

"Alien crafts!"

"What the hell are you talking about?"

"It's simple, there are alien crafts inside this mountain!" She added, "No more talking, we are just below the opening."

Tom looked up, and saw the opening. It faced the mountain next to it, so making it impossible for it to be seen from any angle, other than from where they now stood, "How do we get up there?" he whispered. "It must be at least twenty foot!"

"Closer to thirty," she told him.

"Well whatever it is, how are we supposed to get up there?"

"We're not! Just follow me, and no talking."

Tom did as she instructed. It was getting darker by the second. Margaret kept close to the base of the mountain, "I don't want to be seen!" Tom heard her say.

Tom didn't answer, but stayed close behind. He stumbled on a rock, and fell against the base of the mountain. "Darn it!" he steadied himself, "I'm fine, keep going," he told her, but she was gone! "Where are you?" he whispered. He continued to follow along the mountain base, "Wait," a little louder than a whisper, "Wait for me!"

He heard a noise just ahead of him, it was dark now, and visibility was limited.

"Is that you?" he walked toward the noise, "Why didn't you wait for me?"

"What are you doing here?" It wasn't Margaret! "Who are you? And what are you doing here?"

Tom quickly guessed he had run into the Air base police, "I got lost out here," he lied.

"This is a restricted area!" There was two of them, and they were armed.

"I didn't know that," he lied again. "I'll turn back!"

"No! You will come with us!"

Tom replied, "What for?"

"You can explain your trespassing to the base commander!"

"I told you, I just got lost is all!"

"You can tell that to him," they kept their guns on him, "This way," they ordered.

Tom looked around for Margaret, "Is there someone else with you?" one of the officers asked.

"No. I was just trying to see where exactly I am." Where had she got to? "I'm in the US army," he told them.

"That is of no consequence, you were still trespassing!" They led him away.

Chapter 48

"It's dark, so you can go now!"

Elliot got to his feet, "I'm going," he walked to the window, and looked outside, "No one about out there," Elliot turned away from the window, just then he heard a tapping sound, "What was that?"

Bram had heard it too, "There's someone at the door!"

"I didn't see anyone just now," said Elliot.

"Quickly, get out of here! You can't be seen here!"

Elliot asked, "Where to?"

"Down there," Bram pointed toward the hallway, "into one of the bedrooms!" The tapping again, "Hurry!" Bram waited until Elliot was out of sight, before opening the door. It was Margaret, "What are you doing here?" he asked her.

She pushed past him, "I had to come!"

Bram closed the door, "How did you manage to get back on the base?"

"Margaret, it's you!"

Margaret turned round to see Elliot standing in the doorway, "Elliot, you're here too!"

Elliot walked toward her, "Are you all right?"

"Yes, yes, I'm fine, but.."

"Wait a minute! I asked you a question, how did you get back here?" Bram was angry. Margaret answered, "The same way I came before!"

"Which was?"

"Through the mountain," she told him.

Bram did not believe her, "That's not possible! You would have been seen!"

"It's true!" Margaret looked at Elliot, "I'm telling the truth. No one saw me!"

"I believe her," said Elliot.

Bram replied, "I'm not surprised by that!"

"What is wrong with you? You've become more and more reluctant to help her!"

Elliot's sudden flare up surprised Bram, "Nothing is wrong with me! And I only promised to help her get safely off the base, and I did! But now look, she's back!"

"Don't talk about me as if I were not here!"

Bram told her, "You shouldn't be here in the first place!"

"Just calm down," said Elliot, "This is doing us no good."

"I'll tell you what's doing us no good, her being here!"

"I understand your concerns, but I really don't want to cause any trouble," said Margaret, "I'll tell you what I've learned, and then I'll go."

Bram replied, "Whatever that is, I don't wish to know!" He was tired of all the intrusions, "Just go!"

"I want to hear what she has to say, even if you don't," said Elliot.

Bram told him, "Don't you see, we'll all end up like her friend, if she stays here!"

"He's right," said Margaret, "I've not been totally honest with you about not being seen," she told Elliot.

"I knew it!" Bram went to the window, "She'll get us all killed!" He looked out.

Elliot asked, "You were seen? By whom?"

"The Air base police, I think."

Bram could see no one outside, "They must have followed her here! Now do you see?" he said to Elliot.

Elliot asked her, "What exactly happened?"

"Tom Myers was close behind me, when I heard.."

"Who the hell is Tom Myers?" asked Bram, now even more furious, "You brought someone with you? Are you totally crazy?"

"Take it easy Bram, let her continue," Elliot told him. "Did you bring this Tom Myers with you?" he asked her.

"No I didn't. He was hiding in the back of my car. He had followed me!"

Bram asked Elliot, "And you believe all this?"

"Yes I do. Why should I not?"

Bram shook his head, "I give up. But I'm not taking any risks for her, so she can stay at your quarters! Oh, and where is this Myers guy now?"

"He was caught. The Air base police took him to the Colonel," she told them.

Bram said, "Well that's just great!"

"Calm down," Elliot told him, "he wouldn't give you away, would he?"

"I'm sorry, but I don't know that for sure."

Bram was unable to remain calm, "What *do* you know for sure?"

"He knows about my friend Mark."

Elliot asked, "What is it he knows?"

"That he had been killed here on the base."

"I knew it!" Bram bellowed.

Elliot replied, "We don't know for certain that he will say anything. Who did you say he was?"

Bram said, "She didn't!"

"Let her answer!" Elliot told him. "Who is he?"

"He's the son of Harriet and Frank Myers, they were the couple I told you about."

Elliot asked, "The couple that were killed and mutilated?"

"Yes. Their son Tom, he'd just returned home from Vietnam.."

"He's in the service; the Marines, most probably," said Elliot. "He won't crack so easily!"

"You don't know that for certain!" said Bram. "There's only one person here that witnessed her friend's death, and that's *you*," he told Elliot, "So if I were you, I'd be very worried!"

"He's right, only you knew that Mark was killed," said Margaret, "I should just hand myself in."

Elliot asked, "And say what?"

"I'll say that I followed Mark here, which I did, and tell them that I believe they killed him!"

"You can't do that," Elliot replied. "You didn't see him being killed!"

"I'll say that I *believe* that they did, not that I saw them do it!"

Bram remained at the window, surveying the surrounding area, "You can both decide what you are going to do some place else!" he told them. "I have my own plans, and no one is going to get in my way!" He turned to look at them, "Just go!" Bram had no more patience for either of them, and he certainly had no intention of assisting her any longer. If she was stupid enough to return to the base, well then, she can face the consequences on her own!

"Why are you being like this?" asked Elliot, "It was you that approached me first, asking if I had seen her friend!"

He had only done so, as he had been furious about the Air police putting a gun to his head, he hadn't really cared about finding her friend, "He's dead, and there's nothing anyone can do about it!"

Margaret replied, "I discovered that the only person giving all the orders here, is Colonel Maxwell, that's why I came back, to see that he pays for what he has done! But he's right," she looked at Bram, "I shouldn't have come back here, I'm sorry."

Bram turned away from the window to look at her, "No, you should not have come back here! You said you know for certain that the Colonel is the only one giving the orders around here, how do you know that?"

"He was made commander of this Air base back in.."

"1931," Bram interrupted.

"You knew?"

"Of course I knew," Bram replied.

"So you must know he's the only one in command on this base," she said.

"The only one on the base, yes, but there are others!"

Elliot asked, "What others?"

Bram had said too much, "Look it doesn't matter, I just want both of you out of here!"

"We can go to my quarters," Elliot told her.

"Cozy," said Bram.

Elliot replied, "I don't need your wise cracks!"

"Both of you just get out of here," Bram told them. Elliot and Margaret left Bram's quarters. She could ruin everything! He had waited a long time to be posted to the desert Air base, he would allow no one to mess it up for him now! He checked outside, he could see no one. The night patrols, he knew, would have already begun. Bram was still feeling angry at all the intrusions. Why come to him? He didn't want to know. Her friend was dead, why couldn't she just leave it at that? It was obvious there was nothing she, or anyone else, could do about it. She was so very beautiful though. But beauty wouldn't keep her alive! He had already decided, that he wasn't going to wait around until that Myers guy spilled his guts to his incarcerators. He intended to check around the Air base, and see if he could find out anything for himself, and the holding compound was a good place to start.

He was going prepared. If the Air base police discovered him exploring the base under cover of darkness, he would have a surprise for them! Everything he would need was in the rucksack he carried on his back. Bram surveyed the area surrounding his quarters, before starting out for the holding compound. There was no sign of any police patrols being carried out. Normally he would have heard their jeep pass his quarters at least three times by this time, but he had seen and heard none. Perhaps too busy with their newest prisoner!

Bram made sure to stay in the shadows. He arrived at the compound, and went around to the front of the building. No jeep was parked outside this time. He moved along the wall of the building to the door of the compound. It was locked. A large mortise lock was fixed in place. Maybe he was still being questioned by the Colonel? Margaret had said that they were taking him to the Colonel. He knew exactly where the Colonels quarters were, he had seen it on the map. He headed there.

Chapter 49

"Did you find out anything else?" Elliot asked her, "Besides Maxwell being the only one in command around here?"

Now in Elliot's quarters, Margaret began to tell Elliot what she had found in the newspaper archives, about the name Stephenson and Howard, "I know I've heard that name before," she said.

"Lieutenant Howard, Bram Howard," he told her.

"His father was in the Air Force! He was posted to this base!"

"I knew he had been in the Air Force, and I recall at our first briefing, the Colonel saying that he had known him." 'Elliot told her, and asked, "You said Stephenson, who's that?"

Margaret began to tell Elliot what had happened to Max and the others. She told him about how she had found the sheriff dead, and had gone to see if Max had seen anything.

"And had he?"

"No. He did tell me that the sheriff had let him go with a warning to respect the law in future. He was alive when he had last seen him."

"But what caused the fire? Did they all die?"

"Yes, and with the sheriff now dead, the Mayor is in charge, and well.," Margaret began to cry, "it was awful! There was an explosion and.."

Elliot tried to comfort her, "You don't have to continue if you.."

Margaret interrupted, "It's okay, I'm fine. I need to tell you now, we probably don't have much time!"

"I don't think he will give you up," said Elliot.

"Who?"

"Tom Myers."

"I don't know that for sure. He wants to know who killed his parents."

"I thought the Mayor said it was Max and.."

Margaret didn't wait for him to finish, "But he knows that I don't believe that. I think he believes Mark is the killer."

"But you told him
Mark's dead!"

"I don't think he believes that either," she told him.

"I only hope he doesn't tell them you're here on the base," said Elliot, "but by the sounds of it, I think he will!"

"He doesn't know about you and Bram."

"It won't take long for them to figure out that the only way you could have known about Mark, is that someone here on the base told you!"

"They won't know it was you," said Margaret.

"I think they will, as there were only three people there at the time, and two of them were scientists!"

"I'm so sorry, I never meant for this to happen," she told him.

"It's okay, but it's true we don't have much time, I need to get you out of here!"

"You stay here. I'll go back the way I came."

"No, you can't do that they will be expecting you to go that way," he told her, "they're most probably waiting for you right now!"

"So what should I do?"

"I don't know. I need time to think."

"I've only managed to make things worse! I begged Max to go with the deputies, and just answer their questions but he wouldn't listen, none of them would listen! I took the children.."

"The children you say?"

"Yes, four children. I took them to Mel's house."

"Mel? That's the name you mentioned earlier."

"Yes, Mel Stephenson, his father, Dan Stephenson, had been in the Air Force, and was posted to this base. It was not until I had looked up the names in the town hall records, that it became obvious that something wasn't right."

"What wasn't right?"

"They had all had no children!"

Elliot regarded her with interest, "Dan Stephenson had no children? Didn't you just say that you brought the children to his son Mel's house?"

"That's right, I did!" Margaret answered, "And what's more the Myers never had any children either!"

"So what do you think is going on then?"

"I'm afraid I don't know," she told him.

"What did Tom Myers say when you told him that there was no record of his parents ever having a child?"

She replied, "I didn't tell him that. I just asked if he had been born in another state, as that would explain why I could find no record of his birth in the town's records."

"And had he been born some place else?"

"No. It had been a home birth, he had been born on their farm."

"That is strange," Elliot replied. "Did you talk to Mel about it?"

"No. I went back to Mel's after the fire but they were gone!"

"Gone?"

"Yes, and the children too!"

Elliot thought for a moment, allowing what Margaret was telling him to sink in, "You said there were four children? What did they look like?"

"Yes that's right, four; three girls and one boy. I didn't see them very clearly, it was dark, and when I took them to Mel's they didn't switch on the lights, in case of wakening them," Margaret explained, "but they were all fair haired, with pale complexions.."

"My god!"

"What is it?"

Elliot declared, "I knew he was lying!"

"Who? What's wrong?"

"The children are here, on the base!"

"What? They're here?"

"Yes, they are here, and what's more, the Colonel intends on using them to assist with his experiments!"

Part 5

Revelations..

Chapter 50

"We have to get them off this base," Margaret told him.

Elliot looked at her, he knew she was right, but just didn't know how, "I don't know how we can?"

"Do you know where on the base they are being kept?"

"No, but at a guess, I would say the Colonel would keep them close, and I know where he is!"

"Then we'll go there!"

Elliot was amazed by her courage, "You really want to help them?"

"Of course!"

"You do know the risks, and if we get caught.."

Margaret didn't wait for him to finish, "I know the risks, but I promised to keep them safe. Do you think we should go to Bram's, ask him to help?"

"I don't think there's any point. He won't help," he answered, adding, "And *we* might not be able to help them either!"

"I know, but we have to try!"

Elliot could only admire her pluckiness, "You're right," and her beauty, "we have to try." He cast an eye outside his window, "No patrols. I've only just noticed that."

"Only just noticed what?"

"Well usually by now I would have heard the base police pass here a few times, and I haven't heard them pass once," he told her.

"So why do you think that is?"

"I don't know."

Margaret asked, "How many of them are there?"

"How many what?"

"Base police officers."

"I'm not sure, I've only ever seen the same two officers," he told her. "Why do you ask?"

"Remember I said, when Tom was caught, that I heard one of them say they were taking him to the Colonel?"

"What of it?"

"Well if they are the only two, then they may still be with the Colonel."

"And that's why there's been no patrols," he deduced.

"Yes."

"If that is so, then we should take full advantage and look for the children," Elliot told her. "I know it's unfortunate for that Myers fellow that he got caught, but it might just be lucky for the children that he did!"

"It certainly leaves the path clear for us to find out where they are being held," Margaret added.

"It does, so let's not waste any time and start looking for them!"

"Where are we going to start?"

Elliot replied, "The Colonel's quarters!"

"I do hope you're right, and he is keeping them close by him," said Margaret.

He was captivated by her. There was something about her; something he knew he would never understand, "I do too," and he knew, he would never need to, "But I'm as sure as I can be, and for now, that has to be good enough."

They both stepped into the darkness outside, not knowing what the night would eventually bring.

Chapter 51

"I just saw someone!"

"Where?"

"Just ahead of us," said Elliot, "There! Did you see him?"

"Yes. I did," Margaret answered.

"Couldn't quite make out who it was though," said Elliot. "It's certainly not one of the base police officers."

"How can you be sure?"

"They have no need to hide in the shadows. Whoever it was, he was going in the direction of the Colonel's quarters."

"You think that's where he's going?"

Elliot replied, "It sure looks that way!"

"What are we going to do?"

"We'll follow him."

The man ahead of them moved swiftly and silently. Margaret had a thought, "Do you think it could be Bram?"

"I did think that, but why should he be sneaking about the base, he wants nothing to do with what ever is going on here."

"Maybe he was just saying that," she replied.

"He sounded pretty sincere to me!"

The desert sky was unusually cloudy. "It's so dark now, it's difficult to see him," said Elliot, "I'm not sure where he's gone."

"How far are we from the Colonel's.."

"There he is," Elliot announced, "He disappeared around the back of that building just ahead of us!" Elliot pointed to a large concrete building, about 19ft or so in height.

"I didn't see him," Margaret replied and asked, "How far are we from the Colonel's quarters?"

"That building *is* the Colonel's quarters!"

She asked, "What do we do now?"

"We get a little closer, and then we wait a while."

"Wait? What for?"

"To see what happens," Elliot told her, "We need to know who that guy is, *and* what his intentions are."

"We could be here all night waiting!"

"We'll give it thirty minutes, then we'll make our move," Elliot told her.

"Okay," she answered, following him to the building closest to the Colonel's, where they waited. "Why the mutilations?"

"What?"

"Why were they all mutilated? Why were some of their organs removed?"

Elliot replied, "Oh right, you mean the murders. I don't know."

"Their tongues and eyes were also removed."

"I really have no idea," said Elliot.

"And those crop patterns, what do you think made them?"

"I think we were meant to believe that alien crafts made them."

She replied, "You say that like you know different."

Elliot kept a close watch on the Colonel's building, "I'm not sure what to believe anymore."

"First those crop patterns appeared, and the Myers were killed, then the sheriff, and I'm certain that somehow this Air base has something to do with it."

"I believe it does too," Elliot agreed. "But I also think that there are people outside of this base who are connected to all of these occurrences."

"Like who? The government?"

"No. Not the government," said Elliot.

"If not the government, then.."

"There! Did you see that?"

"What?"

Elliot pointed to the Colonel's building and to one of the windows, "I saw a child!"

"But there are no lights on, how can you tell?"

"It was just a silhouette, but it was that of a small child!"

"Are you sure?"

"Positive," he told her.

"Then they *are* in there," she replied, "We have to get them out!"

"Yes we do. Let's go." They both moved slowly toward the building, and went around back, hoping to find a way inside.

Chapter 52

The Colonel's building was quite large and ornate, which was not unusual for an officer's quarters. Now around the back of the building, "How do we get inside?" asked Margaret in a whisper.

"These old buildings will always provide a way in, other than the front door," Elliot told her. "Check all the ground floor windows," he instructed.

"For what?"

"With the dry conditions of the desert, and the low to zero maintenance on these buildings, we should be able to find one that will be easy to prise open."

Margaret did as he said and began checking each of the windows.

It wasn't long before they found one. "Here's one," said Elliot. "And just big enough to get through."

She hurried over to him, "How can I help?"

"Find me a rock."

Margaret looked around the building, "Will this do?" She handed him the rock.

"Let's hope so." Elliot began to dig at the wall that surrounded the window. Large pieces of concrete fell from around the frame. "It's working," he told her.

"Great!"

"I think maybe, there's just enough space there for us to get our hands in?" he told her.

Margaret looked at the gap he had dug out along the window frame, "Yes, I believe there is," she agreed.

"Put your hands in, and grab hold off the frame with me," he told her.

She did as he instructed. The window frame came away from the wall without much difficulty, and even the glass remained intact. Elliot eased the frame off, and stood it against the wall of the building. "I'll go first," he told her, "and make sure it's safe." He wanted to keep her safe, although he didn't quite know how he could. "I'll be back soon."

"Be careful," she told him, and watched as he disappeared inside. The Air base at night, had a rather sinister feel about it, and she hoped Elliot would return promptly.

"What are you doing here?"

Margaret swung round to see Bram, "It *was* you we saw!"

"We saw? Who's with you?"

"Elliot."

Bram looked at the opening in the wall, "What happened to the window?"

"We prised it off. Elliot has gone inside. What are you doing here?"

"Well you both better get out of here. I don't want either of you messing things up," he told her. "As soon as he returns, get out of here!"

"Why should we? What do you mean by, mess things up?"

"Unless you both want to die along with Maxwell, you had better get out of here fast!"

Margaret stared at him, "The Colonel? Why, what have you done?"

"They are set to detonate in fifteen minutes," said Bram, "and then he will die!"

"What are?"

"Explosive devices."

"Oh my god, no!"

"Don't worry, I'm sure he'll be back before then," said Bram. "He won't want to leave you out here alone for long." It was obvious to him how Elliot felt about her.

"There are children in there!"

"What? How do you know that?"

"Elliot saw one of them at the window!" she told him. "My god what have you done?"

"The children Elliot spoke of?" asked Bram, "Why would he keep them at his quarters? I don't believe it."

"Why not?"

"Because Elliot told me that they were assisting the Colonel with his experiments, so logically they would be kept in the mountain facility, and not here!"

"Logically or not, they are in there, and you are going to kill them!"

Bram wanted the Colonel dead, by whatever means, but was not expecting the means toinclude the death of innocent children, "You wait here, I'll go find Elliot."

"What are you going to do?"

"Help him get the children out!" Just like Elliot had done moments earlier, Bram disappeared inside of the building. Margaret could do nothing now but wait.

Chapter 53

Elliot had been wise enough to bring a small torch with him. Being careful to only switch it on, if he were sure no one was close by to see it. Although this made it difficult for him to move as quickly as he would have liked, nevertheless, it was the safer option. Judging by where he had entered the building, and by the position of the window where he had seen the child, Elliot was able to roughly navigate, and in mostly darkness, in the right direction.

After finding the stairs, Elliot quickly ascended them. When he reached the top, the landing led off to his right and to his left. He needed to go right, he asserted, and switched on the torch. There were two doors on either side of the short hallway. The window where he had seen the child at, was to the front of the building, so he only needed to search the two rooms to his left.

Elliot waited a moment at the first door. He listened at the door for any sound that would announce, that the room was occupied. He heard nothing. Switching off the torch, he took hold of the doorknob, and began to slowly turn it. The sound it made, proclaimed it was badly in need of oiling. There wasn't much time, he didn't wish to leave her waiting outside longer than he had to, and so, against the sound of the doorknob's contesting, Elliot continued on.

Now inside the room, Elliot switched on the torch again. The room was completely empty. Not one piece of furniture was in there, and more importantly, no children either. Elliot quickly switched off the torch, as soon as he realised someone was coming. He had not heard anyone on the stairs, but someone was now on the landing. Elliot stepped back against the wall. He put his ear against it. Whoever it was, he was no longer moving, most probably listening intently for him.

Still listening, Elliot could here no movement from the other side of the wall. Maybe whoever it was, was gone, Elliot thought, and was about to leave the room, when he heard someone ascending the stairs. Whoever it was, was in a hurry and didn't care how much noise they were making. He wasn't gone after all, Elliot could hear him move away from where he had been, and toward the stairway, by his guess.

"What are you doing here?"

Elliot recognised the voice immediately, it was the Colonel's lieutenant!

"Get out of my way or I'll kill you too!"

He recognised that voice too, it was Bram! Margaret had been right, it had been him they had seen disappear behind the Colonel's building earlier. Elliot stayed where he was. He could hear them tussling at the top of the stairs.

"You have no right to be here!"

"Get off me!"

The lights along the hallway and landing came on, "I can take it from here, lieutenant!" It was the Colonel. "So you've known all along lieutenant Howard!"

"Yes I have!"

"I must say, I didn't think you had," said the Colonel.

Elliot heard Bram, "Why? Because I didn't crack when you had those two pissants put a gun to my head?"

The Colonel laughed, "I must confess, I did think you would have, if you had known something."

"I'm going to kill you!"

"I don't see how, you're not in any position to kill anyone lieutenant!"

Elliot had no idea as to why Bram would want to kill the Colonel so badly, nevertheless, it couldn't bes simply be down to the Colonel having killed Margaret's friend. He knew there had to be more it than that! And what was it Bram had known all along?

"Oh, I'm in a better position than you think Colonel!"

"Get him out of here," Elliot heard the Colonel order his lieutenant.

"To the mountain facility Sir?"

"Yes," the Colonel answered.

"Another of your collaborators, I will kill you too!" said Bram.

Elliot could only guess it was the lieutenant that Bram was referring to.

"It doesn't have to be like this, we need each other," said the Colonel. "You only think you know the full story, but I have a few more surprises for you!"

Elliot could hear Bram mumble something, but he could not make it out, and then he heard them descend the stairs.

Margaret, he hoped she had heard the commotion, and had been wise enough to keep out of sight. As soon as it all went quiet, Elliot, after having checked the next room, which he also found to be empty, returned to Margaret.

Chapter 54

Elliot exited the house through the window. "Margaret are you there?" There was no reply. It was very dark and Elliot could not see her. "Where are you?"

"I'm here," Margaret replied.

Elliot jumped to the ground. "Thank goodness you're all right!"

"Who was in there with you and Bram? Where is he?" she asked, "Did you find the children?"

"No children in there." Elliot was surprised she knew about Bram, "How did you know Bram was in there?"

"Where is he? We have to get out of here now!"

"The Colonel has him, they took him to the mountain facility."

"We have to go! Bram placed explosive devices inside of the house!"

"He did what?" Elliot asked, "Did he say when they'd detonate?"

"Fifteen minutes he said, right before he went into the house to look for you!"

"Let's get out of here now!" Elliot grabbed hold of her hand, and they ran from the building, "How long ago was that?"

"When he went in after you," Margaret replied, adding, "About ten minutes ago, or maybe a little more. I'm not sure."

"Just keep running!"

Elliot now sure, they had put sufficient ground between them and the Colonel's building, slowed up, "I think we'll be safe at this distance," he told her. They stopped to look back at the building, "Are you sure he said fifteen minutes?"

"Yes. That's what he said."

Elliot wondered if Bram actually *had* placed explosives in the building, "Then they should have detonated by now."

"But that's what he said," Margaret repeated, "Perhaps he disarmed them?"

"Deactivate," Elliot corrected, "Why would he do that?"

"When I told him that you had seen a child at the window in there, he went in to help you get them out."

Elliot was surprised by this, "He did? But why should he care? He told us he wanted nothing to do with what was going on here. And not just that, there's something else."

"What?"

"When I was in there, I heard Bram tell the Colonel that he had known all along."

"Known what all along?"

"I don't know, but I do know Bram wants the Colonel dead!"

"That's right, he said that to me too, that he wants the Colonel to die. That's why he put those explosives in his house," she told him.

"I knew there was a reason why he refused to help us!"

"Why do you think he wants to kill the Colonel?"

"Not sure, but all along he's been trying to assert who gives the orders around here, and he seemed pretty interested when you told him that the Colonel was!"

"Yes, you're right, he was very interested," she agreed.

Elliot looked back in the direction of the Colonel's quarters, "Should have detonated by now."

"Then he must have deactivated them," said Elliott, adding,

"If there were any explosives in the first place!"

"He seemed pretty genuine to me," she replied. "I think it's likely he did deactivate them when he went back inside."

"Whatever he done back there, there's no explosion to raise any alarm." Now noticing once again, the lack of any night patrols, "And still no police patrols either," even now he thought that to be odd.

"You said they took him to the mountain, that's where Bram said the children would be," Margaret told him. "We have to go there!"

Elliot was afraid she would say that, "That place is a fortress, I don't see how we can get in there without getting caught!"

"We have to try," she urged.

He would have done anything for her, "We might be lucky, the Colonel may well be too preoccupied with Bram, and that Myers fellow they captured earlier." He hoped.

"The children might not be his main concern tonight!"

"If we do manage to find them, and get them off the base, they may not be missed until morning, and we could be long gone by then," she added.

"Yes, well, let's hope so," said Elliot. They headed for the mountain facility.

Chapter 55

Now at the mountain facility, and while the lieutenant secured him to a chair with rope, the Colonel held the gun on him. "I saw them," Bram told the Colonel.

"You saw them?"

"The children," Bram answered, "And I'd wage you're keeping them somewhere in your quarters!"

"My grandchildren," the Colonel replied, "Yes, they are here on the base, what of it?"

"You have to have had *children* in order to have grandchildren," Bram answered.

"So you've been checking up on me," the Colonel laughed. "I'm impressed."

"So where are your two goons tonight?" Bram struggled against the restraints.

"Goons?"

Bram hated them just as much as he hated the Colonel, "The pissants you call police officers!" He intended to get revenge for their little stunt that morning in the holding compound.

"They're otherwise engaged on the other side of this mountain. You see I'm expecting a visitor tonight, might even be here already."

"More of your alien friends?" Bram mocked.

The Colonel smirked, "Of a sort, yes." The Colonel turned to his lieutenant, "Find out where they are, and more importantly, if everyone is here."

"Yes sir," he left.

"Your aliens not good time keepers?"

"Your wise cracks will do you no favours," the Colonel pulled up a chair, and sat opposite Bram, "So you have something against aliens have you?"

"No. I have something against you!"

The Colonel laughed, "I'm certain you do. But do you know *everything*? Now *that* I'm not so sure. Why don't we begin with what *exactly* you do know."

With every bone in his body, Bram wanted him dead, "The only thing you need to know, is that I'm going to kill you!"

"You are beginning to bore me now, lieutenant Howard. Let us begin with your father's untimely death. What happens then?"

Bram became enraged, "You killed him, you son-of-a-bitch!" He tugged harder against his restraints, "I know you did, so don't bother denying it!"

"I was not about to deny it. I mean, what would be the point?"

Bram was surprised by the Colonel's unexpected candour, "So you did give the order?"

"Yes, but you knew that already."

Bram had suspected the Colonel was the one responsible, however hearing him admit it, was still a surprise to him, "Why? Why did you have to kill him?"

"Yes. Let us move on to why," the Colonel stood up, and pushed the chair aside, "Why do *you* think I did? Who was it I actually killed?"

"What the hell are you talking about? You killed him because of what he knew!"

"Who? Who did I kill?"

Bram became even more infuriated with the Colonel, "What do you mean who? My father of course! Why are you playing games? You know who I'm talking about!"

"Your father eh?" the Colonel stared at him intently, "He was not your father!"

"What the hell are you talking about? Of course he was!"

"No. He wasn't," the Colonel repeated.

Bram was confused, what was the Colonel trying to do? "I don't know what your game is, but it won't work on me!"

"Oh, this is no game, I can assure you!"

Then if it wasn't a game, then why was he telling him this? "What are you trying to achieve? You already admitted to killing him."

"Yes I did have him killed. But like I said, he was not your father, well at least not biologically," the Colonel didn't flinch, he kept his gaze on him. "Just as I had expected, you do not know the entire truth." The Colonel remained calm. "But now it's time you did," he told Bram.

Bram didn't trust him. He believed the Colonel would try anything to wrangle his way out of murder, "You killed him! Nothing you tell me will make a damn difference, and it won't change anything, I will still want you dead!"

"Well even serial killers get a defence," the Colonel mocked, "Besides, aren't you even the slightest bit curious as to *who* your real parents are?"

"Parents? Are you now saying my mother is not my mother? You are so fucked up!"

"Why should I make that up?"

"Because you're a sick mother-fucker! You're even going to use those kids in your grisly experiments!"

"Now how could you know that?"

It was too late, it had slipped out in anger. Bram couldn't take it back now, and it wouldn't take long before the Colonel figured out who had told him!

"Sir," the lieutenant returned, "I need to talk to you outside," and he seemed anxious.

The Colonel told him to wait outside, "I'll be back in a moment," he told Bram. "And when I return, you can tell me how it is that you know about those kids." The Colonel left the room. Bram tugged vigorously to get free.

The Colonel had been gone about ten minutes, and Bram had managed to loosen the ropes, only slightly, and not sufficient to free himself. The Colonel was most certainly, the perverted twisted individual his father had told him about. Bram wanted revenge for his father's execution. He pulled and tugged violently on the ropes.

The door opened, a man looked in. Bram had never seen him before, "Who are you? Another one of his goons, I expect!"

He entered the room, "Why are you tied up?"

Bram didn't't expect that question, "What? Who are you?"

"Tom Myers, I came here with.."

Bram didn't't wait for him to finish, "Margaret! You came here with her, right?"

"That's right. But why are you tied to that chair?"

"Never mind that, untie me! Hurry! He'll be back any second!"

Tom went to help Bram, "Who will be back?"

"The son-of-a-bitch that tied me to this chair!" Now untied, Bram hurried to the door, "Did you see anyone?" Bram checked the corridor outside, "It's clear, let's go!"

"Where?"

"I will explain everything when we're well away from this room," Bram told him.

"I killed those two, they didn't't leave me any choice."

Bram realised he was referring to the two base police officers, "They're dead?"

"Yes."

"Good, that saves me from having to do it. Now let's get out of here!"

Chapter 56

"Where do you think he's keeping the children?"

Elliot really didn't know the answer to that, "Hopefully we'll find them in the mountain facility."

"I can't explain it, but I just have a feeling they are not anywhere *on* the base!"

Elliot regarded her with interest, "I had that feeling too, but didn't want to say. I got to thinking that after we left the Colonel's place."

"Me too, how very strange. And there's Mel and his wife, where are they?"

"If they're not here, then where would they be?" asked Elliot.

"I'm not sure, but the feeling is getting stronger, it's as if they are calling to me."

Elliot had not quite felt that, however he did feel strongly that they were some place else.

"What should we do?"

They were close to the mountain facility now, "Maybe we shouldn't go in there just yet," said Elliot. He couldn't tell her that he had a bad feeling about going into the mountain, "We should take a moment to think." They sat on the ground outside one of the base's storehouses, making sure to keep themselves well out of sight.

"I have this terrible feeling about going in there," she looked at the mountain.

"Me too. We'll wait," said Elliot.

"But what about Bram?"

"There isn't much we can to do to help him, without getting caught ourselves. Then who would help the children? They need us!" Elliot was surprised by his own words, and by the sudden urge he felt to get to them, and quickly.

"You're right, they need us. I just wish I knew where they were!"

Elliot knew it was love, having never felt this way about anyone before, "We'll find them," he assured her. "We'll just stay here a minute."

"It's those mutilations, they just don't make any sense," she told him.

"Why do you say that?"

"Why not just kill them, why mutilate their bodies?"

Elliot had thought it odd too, "After you told me about the Myers, I started thinking, and I recalled a pathologist friend of mine, he mentioned that he collects fluid from the eyes to determine the time of death, and also to check for any toxins in the body, like drugs or alcohol. You did say their eyes had been removed?"

"Yes, their eyes, tongues and sexual organs."

Elliot asked, "And no blood was left in the bodies either?"

"That's right. What do you make of it?"

"Not sure, but I don't believe it was the work of devil worshippers, or aliens!"

"Nor do I," she told him.

"So first we had the Myers. You said they had no children, and yet there's Tom."

Elliot tried to make sense of all that had happened, "Then the sheriff. Did he have a family?"

"No. No wife or children."

"Okay. Then there's the children's parents.,"

"They weren't mutilated," she told him.

"Yes, but not much of their bodies would have survived that fire!"

"What are you saying? That someone *wanted* to destroy their bodies on purpose?"

"I think someone wanted to remove something they didn't want found in an autopsy!"

Margaret asked, "Are you serious? Do you really think that could be the reason?"

"Yes, it's the only thing that makes any sense. And we sure don't believe aliens did it? Or devil worshippers?"

"That's for certain!"

Elliot said, "So the question is, what was it they didn't want discovered?"

"Didn't you tell me there are scientists on this base?"

"Yes there are. Why?"

"They would know about the workings of the body, wouldn't they?"

Elliot suspected that they had a lot of hands on experience with bodies, living and dead, "They're all German," he told her. "And old enough to have been young men during the war!"

"What? You think they are the same scientists Nazis' had working for them?"

"Yes I do!"

"Why would they be here on an American Air base? And working for our government?"

"Because they have what our government wants, *knowledge*!"

"But they are guilty of such heinous crimes against humanity!"

"Yes, that's true, but their thinking is, that it's better they are here, and not in the hands of the Russians!" said Elliot.

"So in return for this *knowledge*, the government gives them sanctuary?"

"Exactly!"

"Well I must agree, it makes perfect sense," she answered.

Elliot added, "In executing them, they would loose valuable knowledge. I mean, no one can carry out the kinds of tests they done on living people, and get away with it!"

"But that's not right! They should pay for what they done to all those people!"

"Yes, I agree, and so would millions of others, but *Joe public* don't know they are here!"

"No, and it's all very wrong," said Margaret.

"Yes, it is," Elliot agreed.

"Are you saying that tests were carried out on the Myers, the sheriff, and the children's parents?"

"Perhaps," said Elliot, "You said the Myers had no children, so how is it they have a son? And there's the Stephenson's too, they were also childless. Where are Mel's parents now?"

"Like my parents, they died years ago in an automobile accident. That's it! I remember now!"

"What?"

"The Howards, I saw their records too," she told him, "And there was no record of them ever having had any children either!"

"Bram's parents?" said Elliot, "Maybe that's what he had meant. I heard Bram tell the Colonel that he had known all along!"

"So Bram knows? But what would the Colonel have to do with it?"

Elliot believed the Colonel had everything to do with it, "Somehow all of those childless couples had children, or at least one child, and I reckon the Colonel, and his ghoulish scientists had a hand in it!"

"But what about the sheriff? Where does he fit in all of this? He wasn't married or had any children?"

"I don't know," Elliot replied.

"There's that awful feeling again," she told him.

"What feeling?"

"That we're looking for the children in the wrong place!"

Elliot took her hand in his, "We'll find them," he told her, "I think we should return to the Colonel's quarters though."

"What for?"

"There we may find a clue as to where they are."

"What about the explosives?"

Elliot didn't believe Bram had put explosives inside the building, "If there were any, then they would have detonated by now," he told her.

"Perhaps you're right, there might be some clue as to where he's keeping them."

Elliot and Margaret headed back to the Colonel's quarters in the hope of finding *something* that would lead them to where the four children were.

Chapter 57

Bram and Tom stood at the entrance to the mountain facility. "Good, no one is around," said Bram, "When he finds that I'm gone, he'll return to his quarters."

"How do you know that?"

"Because that's where he's keeping the children, and he's well aware that I know it!"

Tom had no idea what Bram was talking about, he was looking for Margaret, "This is where we part company," he told Bram, "I have to find her!"

"She had nothing to do with the deaths of your parents," Bram told him.

"How do you know about that?"

Bram didn't wish to get into a long conversation about all that had happened, "Look, take my word for it, she had nothing to do with it, and neither did her friend Mark!"

"She said he's dead, is that right?"

"Yes, and so will we, if we don't get a move on!" Bram told him, "The Colonel is the only one responsible for their deaths!"

"And is that where he is now? In his quarters?"

"No, but he soon will be," Bram told him.

"If that's where he is, then that is where I'm going!"

"I have it all set up, and I'm going to enjoy this," said Bram.

"What's set up?

Bram was in no mood to stop and explain everything, "You will have a better chance of surviving if you don't waste time with questions!"

"I can take care of myself," Tom replied.

"Yes, I'm sure you can," said Bram, "and so can the Colonel. Now can I ask you a question?"

"What is it?"

"I noticed you're unarmed, so how did you kill those two?"

"With my two hands," Tom put out his hands in front of him.

"With your two hands eh? Well they must be some pair of hands to take out two armed men!"

"I served in Nam. Just back as a matter of fact."

"So I heard," Bram replied.

"Margaret, right?"

"Right," said Bram. "I'd love to chat more, but I have a Colonel to kill!"

Tom answered, "If he is the one who killed them, then like I said, I'm going with you just to make sure the job's done!"

Chapter 58

"They have been dead a few hours sir," said the lieutenant.

The Colonel looked down at the two dead men, "Didn't you explain to them to exercise caution?"

"Yes sir."

"Bloody fools. Well at least we know *he's* here too," said the Colonel. "Get rid of these bodies lieutenant. I better get back, before someone finds him! And be quick about it, I need you to watch Howard!"

The Colonel left the lieutenant to get on with the disposing of the two bodies. He had been looking forward to this night for a long time, and now it had come, he wanted nothing to go wrong. *Only one*, out of all of them, was now loyal to him. Although he was well aware that loyalty was not built on honesty, as he had not been entirely truthful with him.

The Colonel entered the room expecting to see Bram; he was gone!

"What the hell!" he said aloud, "He's gotten away!" The Colonel was furious. He hurried off to get the lieutenant. Nothing was meant to go wrong! All the planning and preparations, and now it was all about to fall apart. He couldn't let that happen!

"Lieutenant!"

The lieutenant was busy disposing the two bodies, "Sir?"

"Leave that!"

"But you.,"

"Just leave it I said!"

The lieutenant closed the incinerator door, "What is it?"

"He's gone! Howard got away!"

"What do you want me to do Sir?"

"I know where he's gone to," the Colonel told him, "And we had better get there fast!"

"Yes Sir," he switched off the incinerator.

"If he won't comply, then I have no choice but to kill him!"

"But don't we need him Sir?"

"Of course we do, but if I can't convince him, what choice do I have?"

"No other, I guess."

"Out of all of them, he was the most important to me," said the Colonel.

"Yes Sir, I know. Where has he gone to?"

"My old quarters. He's looking for the children," he told the lieutenant. "Let's go, but radio ahead, tell those two to expect company!"

Chapter 59

Tom and Bram had entered the basement, through the same window Elliot had earlier removed. "Are you sure he'll follow us here?"

Bram was certain the Colonel would, "Don't worry, he'll be here. Better get a move on, down here." Bram and Tom went further into the basement. "There's a steel door down there, can't get in there, but here will be fine," Bram told him.

"Fine for what?"

"I positioned some explosives around the building earlier, but had to deactivate them. This one is the only one I need to reset, as they are linked," Bram explained. "When I set this one, it will activate the others. What time do you make it?"

Before Tom could answer, the large steel door at the end of the basement room opened, "What are you two doing here?"

Bram recognised him at once, it was the ground controller that had assisted him on his test flight of the Sabre, the day he arrived on the base. "Where's the Colonel?" Bram asked, stopping what he was doing. He walked toward the ground controller. "Is he back there?" Bram pointed to the room from where the man had just come from.

"This is the Colonel's private quarters, and you shouldn't be here lieutenant." At first Bram hadn't noticed the gun in the ground controller's hand. "You better come with me, I'm expecting the Colonel any minute," he pointed the gun at them. "Hurry!"

Bram and Tom had no choice but to do as instructed, "Where are those hands now?" Bram asked Tom.

Tom understood what he meant, "Don't you worry, I'll have my opportunity!"

Bram replied, "Well make it fast!"

"Stop your talking," the ground controller told them, "In there!"

Bram and Tom entered the room beyond the steel door. There they saw a woman tending to four young children. "These are the two the Colonel's been expecting?" asked the woman.

"He's on his way, so we'll soon know if they are," the controller replied.

The children looked very pale, and may well be quite ill by the look of them, "What's wrong with them?" asked Bram. The large room had two other doors leading off it, and both doors were closed.

"Nothing is wrong with them," the woman answered.

"They look ill to me," said Bram. There were two sets of bunk beds on which the children now lay. "Why keep them down here?"

"We don't have to answer your questions," said the ground controller. He kept the gun on him and Tom.

"Haven't I seen you before?" Tom asked the woman.

"I shouldn't think so," she replied.

"I'm sure I have."

She didn't answer him, but continued to tend to the children.

"I know those kids are not related to the Colonel," said Bram.

The ground controller replied, "That has nothing to do with you!"

"What experiments has he planned for them? I assume you know about them!"

Tom looked at Bram, "What? What do you mean?"

"The Colonel and his Nazi scientists," said Bram, "you wouldn't believe what they get up to, and all in the name of science!"

Tom replied, "What, Nazi scientists? Here?"

The woman stared at Bram, "Do you mind, they can hear!"

"Best they know what you all have planned for them," said Bram.

Tom asked, "What the hell is going on around here? And don't I know those kids? I've definitely seen them before!"

"You most probably have," answered Bram, "They're from that town close by."

"Yeah that's right, they're those hippies' kids!" declared Tom, now recalling where he had seen them before.

"It's nothing to do with either of you who they are!" said the woman.

The ground controller watched them both intently, keeping his gun on them, "Sit over there," he directed them to a bench by the steel door.

Bram spoke to the woman, "So their parents are dead, right?"

"They died in that fire on their farm," Tom told him.

Bram answered, "Yes, I know, but do they know that?" He gestured to the children.

"They have us now," said the woman, "we are their parents now."

"Good god, everyone wants to be their parents! First the Colonel, now you two!" said Bram, "Must be four very special kids!"

"We don't need any of your wise crack remarks," the ground controller answered.

"So why are they here? Their parents were hippies, they would have had nothing to do with the Air Force," said Tom.

"Yes, that is strange," Bram agreed.

The ground controller told them, "Both of you shut up!" They all heard someone approaching; two people by the sounds of it.

Chapter 60

Now at the Colonel's quarters, Margaret asked, "Did you check every room in there?" They cautiously approached the building.

"No, only two of the rooms. There wasn't much point in checking them all, as it was from one of the front windows that I saw the silhouette of a child," he explained.

"And you're still sure that's what you saw?"

"Yes, I'm still sure," Elliot climbed through the window. "Give me your hand."

"I'm getting that feeling again, that they're not on the base," said Margaret.

Now both inside the building, "Well let's hope we find something in here that will tell us where they are," Elliot replied.

"It's so dark in here. How were you able to see anything?"

Elliot took the torch out of his pocket, and switched it on, "I used this earlier."

"Right, good thinking bringing it along."

Elliot shone the torch around the empty room, "That's another thing I found strange when I was here earlier."

"What?"

"There's no furniture!"

"What about the rest of the house?"

"None in any of the rooms I checked."

"That is strange," she replied. "Where should we look first?"

Elliot shone the torch up the stairs, "Up there," he told her.

They slowly ascended the stairs. Half ways up, "There's that feeling again," she said.

"What, the same as before?"

"Yes, but stronger now," she explained. "I feel like I'm close to them, but moving away, and in my mind I'm thinking that they are not *on* the base!"

Elliot thought about what she was saying, "Not *on* the base, but we're close?"

"Yes, that's right. I know it sounds crazy."

"No it doesn't, and I think I know why!"

"Why?"

"They're below us, underground!" Elliot swung the torch round and shone it on the floor at the bottom of the stairs."There must be an underground bunker or basement here," he told her.

"You really think so?"

"Yes I do, and there must be a door on the ground floor that leads to it. Let's go!"

They descended the stairs, "This way," Elliot pointed to the right, "We came that way," he shone the torch to the left of the stairs, "and I didn't see another door."

"You must be right," said Margaret.

"What?"

"About them being underground, here. I feel closer to them now, than I did on the stairs!"

Elliot believed that she must have some kind of psychic ability, "Then you should walk in front, see if you can pick up on where the entrance to the basement is."

"I'm no psychic," she told him, "But I'll try." She walked in front of him, "This way."

Elliot followed closely behind. He wondered, when all this was over, what would happen to them? Would they be together?

However, the bigger question was, would they live to see another day?

Chapter 61

Elliot and Margaret had seen Bram and Tom being taken into the basement room.

Margaret had recognised the man with them.

"Are you sure that was him?"

Margaret whispered, "Yes. I'm sure."

"So he's been working for the Colonel all this time?"

"That's what it looks like, and the children are in there!"

Elliot had never seen the man before, "And he's the one you gave the children to?"

"Yes, him and his wife."

"When you left, they must have taken them straight here," said Elliot, "But why?"

"I don't know," she replied, "How are we going to get them out? Mel has a gun."

"We'll have to wait for our chance," Elliot told her.

"Our chance? I don't see how we are going to get one!"

Elliot would not let her down, "We will, don't worry."

They heard the Colonel and another man, the Colonel's right hand man, Elliot guessed, enter the room.

"Not all here, I see," said the Colonel, "Never mind. Welcome Mr Myers."

There had been no introductions, so how was it the Colonel knew Tom?

"He knows him," whispered Margaret. Elliot nodded.

"Tie them both up," the Colonel ordered.

The Colonel asked, "How was your trip to Vietnam?"

"How do you know me?"

"Oh I know a lot of things," said the Colonel, "Don't I lieutenant Howard?"

"Then you will also know that you're going to die this night!" Elliot and Margaret heard Bram answer.

They heard the Colonel say, "Like I said, they were not your parents Howard."

"They? My mother is alive!"

"Oh that's right, you don't know," said the Colonel, "She had an accident while you've been here. Didn't survive it I'm afraid," he said heartlessly.

"You son-of-a-bitch!"

"Now now lieutenant," said the Colonel, "wait until you've heard the full story."

"What the hell are you talking about?" They heard Bram shout.

"You see, we carried out some experiments some years back," said The Colonel, "And I must say they turned out pretty well, so well in fact, that we were able to carry out the very same experiments only recently."

"What damn experiments?" asked Bram.

Elliot saw the small box in the corner of the room, and crept over to it. "Where are you going?" Margaret whispered. He didn't answer, but instead quietly examined the device. Bram *had* set up explosives after all. "What is it?" she whispered to him.

Elliot crept back to her, "He did set up explosives, and that's one of them," he told her. "I know how it works, so if we have to, I will activate it."

"What for?" Margaret asked.

"We may have to, in order to get away with the children."

"What do you mean?"

"Everyone that knows about those kids is in that room," Elliot told her, "If we get them out, we will have to make sure that no one comes looking for them!"

"The Mayor of that town knows about them," she told him.

"Then we will have to make sure he doesn't come looking for them either!"

"You mean kill him?"

"Whatever it takes," Elliot told her.

"Why do you think those children are here?"

Elliot heard the Colonel speak, "I think we're about to find out," he told her.

"Let's take Tom here," said the Colonel, "Your parents were unable to conceive, so we made an agreement with them."

Tom replied, "You knew them?"

"Yes, I knew them both very well," the Colonel answered, "They took part in our genetics' experiments that would, we hoped, result in a pregnancy. *You* Tom Myers, were the end product!"

Tom replied, "Product! You're a fucking madman!"

Elliot and Margaret heard the Colonel laugh loudly, "That maybe so, but they got the child they always wanted!"

Tom shouted, "So you killed them?"

"Yes, well we had an agreement," the Colonel replied.

"What that they get a child, and in return you have them killed? Some agreement!"

"Why should it bother you, now you know that biologically, they are nothing to you!"

Tom answered, "They raised me, looked after me!"

Bram asked, "So did you have the same agreement with my parents?"

"Yes I did," replied the Colonel, "All they had to do was incubate you all."

Bram replied, "We were not fucking chicken eggs!"

"So who are our biological parents then?" asked Tom.

"The same as mine," Elliot and Margaret heard Mel say.

"Yes, you are all the same, genetically," said the Colonel.

Tom asked, "What the hell does that mean? That we are brothers?"

The Colonel laughed, "In a way, yes, you are!"

Elliot and Margaret listened intently. "Are you hearing all this?" Margaret asked.

"Yes," Elliot replied.

"Let me explain," said the Colonel, "You Howard, why is it you could fly those alien crafts? And you Tom Myers, why is it you can kill so efficiently, and with just your hands? And Stephenson here, he has his own talents too."

Bram asked, "Which are?"

"He talks to aliens, he knows their language," the Colonel replied, "But there's one of you missing. The most important one of all. The one whose children they are!"

Margaret asked Elliot, "Who do you think he's talking about?"

Elliot turned to look at her, "You, he means you!"

"What? Me? My children?"

"It's you! I've known it for quite some time now," Elliot told her, "But there's no time to explain right now," he continued, "I need you to trust me. Do you trust me?"

"I guess so," she replied, "Why, what are you going to do?"

"They have one of the same abilities as you possess. What I want you to do is get close to them, real close, and then simply walk out of here with them. Get as far from this building as you can."

"That doesn't make any sense! The Colonel won't allow me to walk out with them!"

"Just trust me, and do as I've said," he told her.

Elliot stood up, "She's here sir!" he shouted to the Colonel.

"What? What are you doing?"

"Just trust me," Elliot told her.

Chapter 62

"Ah, here she is now," said the Colonel. "Sergeant Dayton, or should I say, Mr Anders. What took you so long?"

"Anders?" said Margaret.

Bram hollered, "Didn't I say he couldn't be trusted?"

Anders pushed Margaret into the room, almost knocking her off her feet, "Shut up," he told Bram. "She was hiding out there," Anders told the Colonel.

"Well we have you all here now," said the Colonel. "And what a reunion this is!"

Bram shouted to Anders, "So you've been working for him all along?"

"Yes, as a matter of fact, I have," replied Anders. "You're all nothing more than a bunch of freaks!" He looked at Margaret.

"Why? I trusted you," said Margaret, feeling deeply betrayed.

The Colonel told her, "He's definitely one of ours Miss. You see, his father is a member of a very unique group. Isn't that right Bill? How is your father now? Still in a coma after that heart attack?"

"Yes, I'm afraid so Colonel," Anders replied. He turned to Margaret, "I'm not an airman either," he told her.

"You set us up!" Margaret looked at the children, "What's going to happen to them?"

"*Your* children," replied the Colonel.

"My children? How can they be mine?"

"We had your eggs removed when you were a child," the Colonel answered. "And with our scientists' knowledge and expertise, along with some genetic modifications, here they are!

And they are amazing too! Oh, and before you ask, *yes* I did have the same agreement with your parents," the Colonel told her.

"None of you are *entirely* human," Anders told them. "You have all been genetically engineered, and from *alien* DNA!"

"What the fuck are you talking about Dayton, or whoever you *really* are?" said Bram.

"Oh it's true," Anders replied. "I have seen the test records of all your predecessors."

"Predecessors?" asked Margaret. She went toward the children, "And they are *my* children." She felt their fear.

"Yes, but *they* your, predecessors, unfortunately didn't survive. A simple cold was all it took for some of them," the Colonel answered. "But now you have evolved, and are able to fight off viruses like most humans can."

"We *are* human!" said Margaret.

"Not entirely," the Colonel reminded her.

Margaret asked the man she had known as Elliot, "How long have you known?"

"I've always known," he told her. "My father has been involved right from the beginning, and the other honourable members."

"I knew there must have been others controlling operations on this base!" said Bram.

Tom asked, now trying to grasp the situation, "And all this for what purpose?"

"We don't have to be enemies," said the Colonel. "I mean none of you any harm. All we have to do is work together."

"Work together? For what?" asked Tom.

"Why should we? You killed and mutilated the people closest to us! The people we knew as our parents, and loved dearly!" said Margaret.

"They were contaminated anyway," said the Colonel. "That's why we had to remove the contaminated tissue and blood."

"I don't believe you!" said Margaret. "I believe you wanted to get rid of them because of what they knew!" Mel had remained silent throughout. "Do you believe all this?"

Margaret asked him. "And you Lori, why are you helping them?"

"We can't have children of our own," she replied. "And Mel wants to.."

Margaret interrupted her, "You think they won't kill you too?"

Lori looked at Mel, "Mel has agreed to cooperate, so I'm going to stand by him," Lori answered. Lori walked over to Mel, and stood by his side. While everyone's attention was on them, Margaret took the opportunity to get closer to the children. The children lying on the top bunks, sat up and moved to the lower bunks instinctively. They were all now huddled together.

The Colonel said, "You can all do the same. Just cooperate like Stephenson here, and who knows what we could achieve!"

"So we all just agree to be your guinea pigs and you will let us live?" said Bram.

Tom said, "Not much of a choice!"

"No chance," Bram replied. "I will kill you first," he told the Colonel.

"You killed my friend," said Margaret.

The Colonel looked at her, "He was trespassing!"

"That's not a reason to kill him!" she answered.

"He had served his purpose," replied the Colonel.

Margaret asked, "And what was that?"

"He got you here!"

"So what about those crop patterns?" she asked him.

"They were nothing to do with us," the Colonel replied. "But the crafts that made them are now in our possession. But Stephenson here," he pointed to Mel, "done a great job convincing your friend that the patterns had hidden messages in them," he laughed loudly. "*You* lured Mark here?" she asked Mel. "You knew he would be killed?"

Margaret couldn't believe what she was hearing. It had all been a set up right from the start! "And what about Max and the others? Why did you have to kill them?"

"That was my lieutenant's handy work," the Colonel replied. "Isn't that right?"

The lieutenant said nothing. "Come on lieutenant, that was some nice flying, and with only one chance at it, you successfully hit the target!"

Bram asked, "You used an air to ground missile? From what aircraft?"

"The F-102," replied the lieutenant.

"Under your orders?" Bram asked the Colonel.

"Of course," he replied.

"Where is she? And the children?" Lori shouted. "They just disappeared!"

The Colonel replied, "Not just extraterrestrial that one, but extra-dimensional!"

"What?" Lori asked, "What do you mean?"

"I've seen her do that before," said Tom.

"I'll go," said Anders. He made for the door.

"Get them back here!" the Colonel told him. "She can't keep it up for long, she will have to reappear soon!"

Bram said, "So that's how she was able to get onto the base without ever having been seen!" He then laughed.

Anders quickly went after her, leaving the Colonel, with Bram, Tom, Mel and his wife Lori, in the basement.

Part 6

A New Beginning..

Chapter 63

Anders ran through the building. He climbed through the same window as before.

"Margaret, where are you?" He could see no one. He ran further from the building.

There she was, just ahead of him. She was carrying one of the children, the youngest, he guessed. Another held her hand, while the other two followed close behind.

He shouted to her, "Margaret!"

She turned to look at him, but did not answer. There was a huge explosion, and he saw her fall to the ground, the children too, were knocked off their feet.

He on the other hand, had been expecting the explosion, and was able to keep on his feet. He hurried to them. "Are you all okay?"

"Get away from us!" Margaret told him, "You lied to me! You were involved in all of this all along!"

"Yes, but I couldn't tell you," he explained, "I needed to be sure first!"

"What are you talking about?"

"You see I didn't know what was going on until my father took that heart attack," he explained, "I found all of his personal files, and discovered that he was part of an *elite* group," he told her.

"Why should I believe anything you say?"

"Because it's the truth!"

Margaret looked past him, and saw the Colonel's quarters burning, "What happened?"

"I reactivated the device Bram set up."

"But why? Did he and Tom get out?"

"No, I'm afraid they didn't. They're all dead."

"Why?" Margaret got to her feet.

"Are they okay?" He looked at the children, "Are you all alright?" he asked them.

"They're fine," Margaret answered.

"Are you sure? Don't they speak?"

"They speak plenty," she told him. She helped each of them to their feet.

He asked, "Where will you go?"

Margaret replied, "I don't know yet, but far away from here for a start!"

"I'm sorry I didn't tell you. I wanted to," he explained, "I'm sorry Bram and Tom died in that explosion, but it was the only way!"

"What are you talking about?"

"Someone would have gotten it out of them."

"Gotten *what* out of them?"

"That you and the children had escaped!"

"Doesn't your father's *elite* group know about them?"

"My father is finished, he's in a coma," he told her. "And as for the rest of them, I will make sure they believe you all died in that explosion!" The base alarm sounded.

"We don't have much time!" he told her.

"Why would you do all that for me?"

"Because I've always hated my father, and when I discovered what he, and the Colonel were doing here, I wanted to stop them!"

"I'm not sure I believe you," she answered. The children huddled close to her.

"Look! They know who you are. They are special, real special!"

"They are staying with me!"

"Of course, and I promise to do all that I can to make sure that they do!"

She held the children close.

"And there's another reason," he told her.

"What?"

"I love you," he saw the surprise in her face, "I know what you're thinking, but it's the truth. I love you, and have done since the moment I saw you!"

"But aren't I just a freak to you? Not *entirely* human!"

"I just said that back there for the Colonel's benefit!"

"But it's true though, isn't it?"

"That you have been genetically engineered from another intelligent species other than a human? Yes."

"You can't even bring yourself to say it!"

"The word *Alien* to me, is not an apt name," he answered. "Look at you, *and* them, you're all so beautiful! Please believe me."

"And where is it you think we should go?"

He was delighted to hear her ask that, as it meant she was at least *beginning* to trust him, "Let me sort things out here. There will be a lot of questions to be answered."

"What will you say?"

"I'll say that Howard flipped and blew up the Colonel's quarters, taking all of you with it!"

Margaret replied, "But that group knows that you were here!"

"Anders *too* is dead! He died in that explosion."

"And they will believe you?"

"Obviously they won't hear it from me, but that will be the news they receive from the base commanders after I give them my report on what occurred here tonight!" He looked around, "You had better get out of here. Soon this place will be swarming with Air men and police!"

"Where do we go?"

"Go back the way you came," he instructed, "There's a house about three miles south of here. Follow the signs for *Desert Rock Trail,* until you come to a house. You will find a key under a pot at the back door. Go inside and wait for me. There is plenty of food there for you and the children. All of you will be safe there," he assured her.

"It sounds like you had all this planned," said Margaret.

"Yes I did," he told her, "but we can talk more about that later. Right now you all need to get out of here!" Margaret did as he instructed. He watched her and the children disappear in front of his eyes. He couldn't wait to be with her again.

Chapter 64

It was well after dawn before he joined them at the house.

"So what do I call you?" Margaret asked.

"Elliot, Elliot Dayton."

"But won't your family look for you?"

"Like I said last night, Bill Anders died in that explosion," Elliot replied.

"Why should they believe that?"

"Because I left a message for the group, saying that I intended to take my father's place, and go out to the base to oversee Mission 5."

"That's what they called it?" Margaret asked him.

"Yes."

"And why were the children living with Max and the others?"

"The only way to hide children who are as extraordinary as these are, was to put them with unusual parents," he told her, "and it certainly made it easier when it came to getting them back!"

"Yes, and it made it easy for them to turn a bigoted sheriff against them too! And why was he killed?"

"The group liked the idea of blaming the killings on the hippies, so all they had to do was sow the seed with the sheriff, convince him that they were in fact devil worshippers," he explained. "Then kill the sheriff."

"They had it all worked out right from the start?"

"Yes, every detail," said Elliot.

"And I can trust you?"

Elliot took hold of her hand, "Yes, and I will do everything to protect you, and the children," he promised her.

"The one responsible for killing Mark is now dead," said Margaret.

"At least he paid in the end," Elliot replied.

"It won't bring him back though."

"Nothing will, but we saved the lives of four innocent children," he told her, "We saved them from a life of tests and experiments or perhaps worse!"

"This elite group you spoke of, what about everything they have done?"

Elliot replied, "They are too powerful. There's nothing we can do."

"They will grow old and die anyway, I guess," said Margaret.

"That won't matter, as their children, and their children's children will take their place! What we need to do is prove to the world that they exist."

"How?"

"Well you're a journalist, and there's no reason why I can't continue working on the base," he told her. "Together we can collect as much as we can about the group, and the desert base!"

"I can't return to the newspaper, I'm supposed to be dead, remember?"

"You won't need to return there," he took her hand, "My Greta is not dead."

"Who?"

"You," he answered. "I meant what I said last night; I have loved you since to moment I met you."

"I had the same feelings when I met you," she revealed.

Elliot could only have dreamed of hearing her say that, "I will take good care of you and the children," he promised.

She knew he would.

Chapter 65

Greta had been gone now for almost two years. He had kept his promise to her. The children had long since grown, after having been given the opportunity to develop their exceptional abilities within the safety of their mother's guardianship. Elliot's and Greta's work was complete. However, there was one last thing to do; to let the world see all that was possible. The truth to their continued existence. Humans were not the only intelligent life in existence, and Elliot had the living proof. All four of them, now too powerful to be caged like animals, or tested like laboratory rats! He and Greta had recorded everything they had learned and discovered over the years. They had also penetrated the elite group, gathering knowledge about their activities.

Elliot had set the scene. He had made sure *they* would find out who he really was, and what had really happened that night on the base. He was well aware that all the members of the elite group from back then, had all since grown old and died, but their eager descendants had taken their place. The 'Blue Files' as he and Greta had named them, would soon be revealed for all the world to see!

The conference would take place on the other side of the world, but the files would get there on time. Elliot was sure of that. He had an image in his head of how the proceedings would go. He and Greta had waited a long time for that moment, even though neither he, nor Greta, would ever live to see it. Elliot checked the time, he guessed he would only have an hour or so to live. He was prepared. He was ready to be with his beloved Greta. He made the lemonade, and took his seat. Not long now.

Chapter 66

The World Conference was taking place in Geneva. Crowds had gathered to see the most powerful and influential men and women arrive. Security was tight, and only those invited were allowed into the conference hall. The usual regulations had been put in place for the event. However, there were some that were *unusual*. It had been stated clearly, that all those invited to take part in the conference were, under no circumstances, to take with them into the conference hall, any files or paperwork. Those carrying computers would have to leave them with security before entering the building. And all speeches prepared by the delegates, had to be handed in at least two weeks prior to the conference taking place, and no speech could be altered thereafter.

Everyone had taken their seats, and the large conference room was filled with the resonant sound of hundreds of people all chatting together. There was a record turnout for the conference because of the rumour that some files, known as *The Blue Files*, would show up at the conference. The files supposedly proved without a doubt, that there *was* intelligent life on other planets, and that they had, and were still, visiting this planet. These top secret files would also prove, that a powerful group of the richest men in the world, were underhandedly controlling world economies, politics, population growth, and worse still, that they had knowledge of pending disasters, but did nothing to warn those in danger.

There was an air of excitement in the hall, as a man stepped up to the podium, "Now ladies and gentlemen, if you are all ready we will begin," he told them, "But first let me put to rest a certain rumour that has been circulating regarding this year's conference. We are not here to discuss E.T!" The hall reverberated with the sound of laughter. It was a few minutes before the man regained the hall's attention.

"This year's World Conference is also being aired live to the rest of the world," he reminded the audience. There was silence once again, and he continued, "The emphasis of this years discussions as you all know *is* Biology's Emergence and Potential. So let us welcome our first speakers who are renowned the world over, as *the* most leading scientists in this field." Loud sounds of applause filled the hall as the highly respected group, consisting of three women and one man, took to the stage. They stood together next to the microphone.

One of the three women spoke, "Good morning ladies and gentlemen," she said, "My name is Butterfly," she stepped aside.

"Hello everyone, my name is Light," said the second woman.

The third woman now spoke into the microphone, "And my name is Umi."

The man now took his turn, "Hello ladies and gentlemen, my name is Eden."

The three women subsequently joined him at the microphone, and together they spoke, "We are the *B.L.U.E* files," they told everyone gathered for the conference. Immediately the hum of people chatting returned to the hall. Eden addressed the conference, *"The Conduit is here."* The room fell silent. The entire world also watched and listened to what they had to reveal. It was beamed to every nation, *live*. There would now be, from that moment on, a *new* world order!